Alexander Balloch Grosart

English Jacobite Ballads, Songs and Satires, etc.

From the MSS. at Towneley Hall, Lancashire

Alexander Balloch Grosart

English Jacobite Ballads, Songs and Satires, etc.
From the MSS. at Towneley Hall, Lancashire

ISBN/EAN: 9783744787956

Printed in Europe, USA, Canada, Australia, Japan

Cover: Foto ©Andreas Hilbeck / pixelio.de

More available books at **www.hansebooks.com**

The Towneley MSS.

ENGLISH
JACOBITE
BALLADS, SONGS & SATIRES,

etc.

FROM

THE *MSS.* AT TOWNELEY HALL, LANCASHIRE.

EDITED, WITH INTRODUCTION, NOTES AND ILLUSTRATIONS,

BY THE REV. ALEXANDER B. GROSART,

ST. GEORGE'S, BLACKBURN, LANCASHIRE.

PRINTED FOR PRIVATE CIRCULATION.

1877.

One hundred copies only.]

CONTENTS.

iv   *Contents.*

Contents.

TO

THE REV. J. W. EBSWORTH, M.A.,

MOLASH VICARAGE, ASHFORD, KENT.

EDITOR OF "CHOYCE DROLLERY" (1656); "MERRY DROLLERIES"
(1661, 1671, 1691); "WESTMINSTER DROLLERIES" (1671, 1672);
"THE BAGFORD BALLADS."
ETC., ETC., ETC.

MY DEAR SIR,

I owe you right hearty thanks for many
a mirthful hour, when fagged and worn, from your
" Drolleries "— your's in inevitable association " for
all time "— many a bright and pleasant hour from
your vivid and daintily-wrought original as distinguished from your editorial writing — many a happy
and transfigured hour from your chatty, over-flowing,
matterful letters, and a deepening sense of privi-
lege in forming your personal acquaintance as
Author, Editor, Artist, Etcher and Engraver, and
generous helper of your fellow-workers. We met
in the grand national Library and were mutually
"taken." I feel sure that the years of the future—
fewer or more — will bind us closer together by
manifold bands. Accept kindly the dedication of
this second volume from the *Towneley MSS.* I
inscribe your name in the spirit of the elder Epistle-
Dedicatory Writers, loving the old ways and the old
fervours. It isn't form, but reality with which I rest,

My DEAR SIR,

Yours faithfully,

ALEXANDER B. GROSART.

St. George's Vestry,
  Blackburn, 26th December, 1876.

PREFACE.

THE *MSS.* from Towneley Hall, Lancashire, printed in the present volume to which I have given the title of *English Jacobite Ballads, Songs, and Satires, etc.*, were another of the FINDS of R. B. KNOWLES, Esq., as Commissioner of the "Royal Commission on Historical Manuscripts," in the "Fourth Report" of which he gives a valuable and substantially careful enumeration of the various pieces preserved therein as part of his "Report" on the Towneley Manuscripts. The very considerable space devoted to the details of these Ballads, Songs, and Satires, &c., may be accepted as declarative of the Royal Commissioner's estimate of their historical value.

As in the *Spending of the Money of Robert Nowell,* —the first Towneley volume, but far beyond it in kind and permanence of interest—I reproduce the whole *literatim et punctatim.* Integrity of text I must ever hold to be the prime obligation of an Editor. At the close I have added Notes and Illustrations so far as was deemed expedient. It had been very easy to enlarge these, and in sooth the temptation was strong, especially with alluring offers

b

from the good friend to whom I dedicate the book, the
Rev. J. W. EBSWORTH, M.A., Molash Vicarage, Ashford. As it is, I have only lightly drawn on his
or COLONEL CHESTER's fecund stores or my own.
Perchance, hereafter, with the Ballads, Songs, and
Satires for the HOUSE OF HANOVER and against the
Stuarts, in a companion volume — most certainly a
historical *desideratum* — I may utilize his and my
own abundant collections. As in the *Spending of
the Money of Robert Nowell*, I have very cordially
to thank the TOWNELEY Family for the long use
and graciously-put permission to print these *MSS.*
I regret that Colonel TOWNELEY has died since the
loan and permission were given.

ALEXANDER B. GROSART.

INTRODUCTION.

—

FROM contemporary "Histories" (so-called) of the
Scottish Rebellions of 1715 and 1745 in Prose and Verse
—among the latter shrewd and quaint DOUGALL GRAHAM'S
now seldom-seen little tome—from the elaborate narratives
by ROBERT CHAMBERS and the still more ambitious "History" of Scotland by Dr. JOHN HILL BURTON—whose
Lives of FORBES of Culloden and Lord LOVAT long preceded it—and from many other less or more historically
trustworthy books as JOHN HOME'S Account and Dr. DODD-
RIDGE'S Life of Colonel GARDINER, as well as from family
biographies and monographs, and gradually accumulating
discoveries and recoveries of national and local *MSS.*—it
is not at all difficult to arrive at a tolerably vivid idea of the
Men and the Events of these periods. Thither the student-
reader will turn in his examination of the various problems
historical and ethical started by "the Rebellions," and that
romance in the eighteenth century after the type of the Age
of Chivalry, the yearning of the heart of Scotland toward
the old line of Kings, not without response in England.
The sentiment in itself was not without a certain nobleness
and pathos. The heather was on fire ; and I for one have no
words of contumely for "the Highlanders" in the knowledge that whatever "Bonnie Prince Charlie" ultimately
became, *certes* in his radiant youth he must have had an
electric winsomeness, while at his worst he was better than
"the Georges" at their best. I say this the more readily
that I regard it as a national benediction that the Stuarts,

whether as James or Charles III. (as I suppose he would
have been named), were not "restored."

The present *MSS.* show with what very humble weapons
—in so far as English poetry is concerned—the "cause"
was fought. Placed beside the pseudo-Stuart Poems of
ROBERT BURNS earlier and Sir WALTER SCOTT, and
JAMES HOGG and ALLAN CUNNINGHAM later, and WIL-
LIAM LAIDLAW, Lady NAIRN, and other minor Scottish
singers still later, and the finely-touched verse-memorials
of WILLIAM WORDSWORTH and Lord MACAULAY, these
the actual utterances look mean and poor. I am bound
also to believe Professor BLACKIE'S laudation, of ALEX-
ANDER MACDONALD as "to the Rebellion of 1745 what the
songs of KORNER and ARNDT were to the Liberation war of
the Germans in 1813" ("Language and Literature of the
Scottish Highlands," 1876.) So too with other Gaelic-writ-
ing "Bards." But taking these present Towneley *MSS.* as a
full and representative collection of English-proper Verse in
behalf of the Stuarts, much cannot be said in praise. All
the more do these *MSS.* bear witness to the profound hold
that "The Prince" took of Scotland at least, and of considerable breadths of England. A *sentiment* must be semi-omnipo-
tent that such humble inspiration sustained and constrained
to so magnificent self-sacrifice.* But here and now it were
out of all proportion to enter on a discussion either of facts
or actors involved, *e. g.,* the accusations throughout of bondage and corruption and oppressive taxation under the House

---

* Professor Blackie, as before, has not translated so much as one would wish
of the '15 or '45 Gælic-poems. But here is one stanza from a song in praise of
the tartan that reminds one of the later-uttered pathetic devotion of one of
Napoleon's Old Guard concerning him :—

> " Let them tear our bleeding bosoms,
> Let them drain our latest veins ;
> In our hearts is Charlie, Charlie,
> While a spark of life remains."

The Napoleon sentiment is in many elements parallel with Scotland's for
Prince Charles.

of Hanover, and the large counter-promises of civil and religious liberty, purity in manners and relief in taxation if only
the Stuarts were "restored," and the Bourbon-like holding
of every one who did not sacrifice everything for "the
cause" to be "traitors" and ingrates—witness the heading
of the poem at page 84 as to the Earl of KILMARNOCK:
and cognate matters would require ample space for their
adequate handling. Ours is a contribution of lowly but
genuine materials toward a clearer insight into the principles
at issue. I use the word "genuine" advisedly; for the
more I study such books as JAMES HOGG'S *Jacobite
Relics* (1st and 2nd series) and kindred collections, the
more I am satisfied that with scarcely an exception the
Ballads and Songs have been so dealt with by their (pro-
fessed) "Editors" as to be virtually modern-antiques, that
is to say, are so changed or added to or "improved" as to
be un-historical, un-authentic, and illusory. Your men of
genius such as SCOTT and HOGG and CUNNINGHAM were
the very last men to be entrusted with such work. In a
sense they indeed give us much that is better (poetically)
than the real originals; but none the less is the imposture
to be condemned and deplored. Hence *(meo judicio)* the
value of such *MSS.* as those of the present Volume, wherein
we have the *ipsissima verba* of the *English Jacobite Ballads,
Songs, and Satires, etc.,* as written down for private circulation among the English adherents of "the Prince." Ours
is indeed exactly such a recovery as HOGG intimated in the
Introduction to his "First Series" when he expressed his
anxious desire to obtain others that (as he said) "had been
confined to the select social meetings of the confirmed
Jacobites, or *hoarded up in the cabinets of old Catholic
families,* where to this day they have been preserved as their
most precious lore." He adds, "Many of these beloved
relics have been given up to me with the greatest liberality;
*yet I have every reason to believe, that in some distant coun-
ties numbers still remain:* for a locality prevails in many of

them, that gives them an interest only in certain families and districts" (p. viii).

In the Notes and Illustrations I point out such of the present *MSS.* as have before fugitively or in out-o'-the-way and long-forgotten books been printed. Even in such cases the Towneley *MSS.* furnish better texts, *e.g.*, the well-known "Towneley's Ghost"—in large paper copies given in fac-simile — is, for *the first time*, accurately printed. From HOGG to DR. CHARLES MACKAY easily-discerned blunders have been perfunctorily repeated. So in other instances. But a very large proportion of these *Ballads, and Songs, and Satires*, appear (it is believed) for the first time.

I have now to notice certain little points promised in the Notes and Illustrations — taking them in the order of the Notes and Illustrations.

1. WILLIAM, DUKE OF CUMBERLAND. Note p. 177, st. 2, l. 3, *Duke Billy.* It must be conceded (*meo judicio*), that while this notorious "Duke" was personally cruel and vengeful to very wantonness, as against the Scottish "rebels," he only executed the (English) national demand. When the bloody vengeance was taken and tidings of the *mode* of it and its thoroughness, there was inevitable revulsion ; and then the nation made Cumberland its scape-goat. That is to say, those who had hounded him on sought uneasily to transfer to their mere tool — a cast-iron one rather than steel — their own culpability. "Duke William" had the nation in the outset with him. Later it execrated where before it had hosannaed—and one has a sneaking kindness toward the man who, when he stood almost alone, held to the "military necessity" of his conduct.

2. MARSHALL WADE. *Ibid*, l. 3. The great Highland "roads" made by this somewhat imbecile "Marshall" are his one good service. Even the bathos of their celebration in the well-known couplet :

> " If you had seen this road before it was made
> You'd have lift up your hands and bless'd General Wade."

has not blotted out his claim on remembrance.

3. SIR JOHN COPE. *Ibid.* l. 4. The Jacobites were never weary in their raillery of this redoubted Knight, whose "sleeping" becomes rather mythical on investigation. On the occasion of her Majesty's first visit to her Scottish Capital, it so chanced that the Lord Provost over-slept himself and was "too late" to receive the Queen. This led to many parodies on the Sir John Cope ballads; and indeed it has been thus utilized over and over with considerable effectiveness, *e.g.*, in municipal and parliamentary elections. Throughout, the incapacity of the Hanoverian "commanders" is dwelt on by the Jacobites with severity if not always truthfully. Easily accessible authorities contain biographical notices of Cumberland, Wade, Cope, &c., &c., so that it does not seem needful to give such here.

4. ARTHUR, LORD BALMERINO. Note p. 179, *A Speech*, &c. The Stuarts, like the Bourbons, deemed no sacrifice for them anything else than bare duty. Hence, the slightest faltering or self-regard took the uttermost name of "treason." It is profoundly noticeable, that even the men who "died" on the scaffold and by the headsman were maligned on the most frivolous grounds and by suspicions born of stupid selfishness. His "graceful partner" was no doubt his companion in death.

5. VERS SUR LE PRINCE EDÜOARD. I had thought of translating the whole, but the "free rendering" of part at page 89 may suffice. These Verses reflect the sorrowful indignation and disappointment of the Jacobites. For France to fail after "the word of a king" was as though the skies had fallen.

6. *The Tears of Scotland*, p. 27. For various readings herein, I find I must content myself with a reference to the text in the collective Works of Smollet. A tradition runs, that the final stanza was added by its author on being remonstrated with for the prior portion — his cheeks being all wet with tears while he wrote it. The hideousness of the Hanoverian vengefulness maddened some of Scotland's

noblest, if not into Jacobitism, into heart-hatred even to loathing of the Georges.

7. *U. D.*, p. 32. I read these letters as U. D. where they occur in the *MS.*, but I cannot be sure that I am correct, neither can I explain them. They cannot denote the Author.

8. *Townley's Ghost*, p. 82. In large paper the *fac simile* speaks for itself. A comparison of our text with all previous will shew how important a contribution to the Jacobite ballads it is. In Hogg (second series, p. 187) it is headed nonsensically "Towly's Ghost"; and in all the collections that I have examined, in st. 3, l. 1, the reading is "Imbrued in bliss" for our "Embowered in bliss": and so with others. Hogg annotates thus: "I copied this song from the Honourable Miss Rollo's papers; and though I got several other copies, yet the name in them all was Towly. I, however, find no such name among those who followed Prince Charles. There was a Colonel Francis Townley, who led the 200 men that joined the Highland army at Manchester, and who was after taken at the surrender of Carlisle, and executed with the rest."

I am indebted to my friend Mr. W. A. ABRAM of Blackburn for the following most interesting details on *the* Towneley whose "ghost" is celebrated in the ballad :—

" Francis Towneley was the fifth son of Charles Towneley, Esq., of Towneley Hall, in the county of Lancaster; and nephew of Richard Towneley, who was concerned in the Jacobite rising of 1715. He was born in 1709. 'His education,' writes the historian of *The Foundations of Manchester*, 'was suitable to his birth, but by some misfortunes in his family he was obliged to retire to France, which happened in the year 1728. Being a man of spirit, he was soon taken notice of by the French court; and being recommended to the King of France as a person capable of a post in his army, Mr. Towneley received a commission, in consequence of which he served

at the siege of Philipsburg, under the Marshal Duke of
Berwick, who lost his life before the walls of that place.
Mr. Towneley, then a young officer, behaved himself there
with such courage and conduct as gained him the respect
and esteem of all the officers in the army. He executed
all the orders of his superiors with the greatest intrepidity,
and exposed himself on every occasion in such a manner
as if life were of no signification when honour and the
service of his master stood in competition with it. He
was likewise in several other sieges and engagements,
where his behaviour was always such as became a man
of honour ; and as he received the pay of the King of
France, he thought it his duty to serve him with all the
fidelity he was capable of. Afterwards he came into
England, and resided privately in Wales upon a small
income till about the time of the Rebellion. The French
King, imagining Mr. Towneley might be of service in pro-
moting his views in the invasion which he had meditated
against Great Britain, sent him a colonel's commission,
to enable him to raise forces, and to assist his ally, the
Pretender, in his expedition to Scotland.'

"In the beginning of November, 1745, Prince Charles
Edward Stuart, who had reached Scotland from France
three months before, and in the interval had raised a force
of several thousand partizans, entered England. After
a brief resistance he occupied Carlisle, where he remained
several days. Several of the English gentry joined his
standard there. On November 24th the Prince and his
army reached Lancaster. The number of the insurgents
was about 5,600 men, chiefly Highlanders. On the 27th
of November the Prince appeared at Preston. Francis
Towneley probably joined the Prince on his march from
Lancaster to Manchester. On November 20th, at Manchester, the contingent of Lancashire recruits joined. It
numbered only 300 men, some of whom had been brought
by Francis Towneley from the neighbourhood of Towneley

and Burnley. Prince Charles gave to Francis Towneley
the command of this detachment. On Sunday, November
30th, the troops of the Chevalier marched to the Collegiate
Church, where certain clergy of Jacobite sympathies conducted the service. Service being over, the Manchester
Regiment were paraded in the churchyard by Towneley,
their colonel. Next day the rebel army moved on towards
Macclesfield, the Manchester Regiment having started on
Sunday night and leading the van. In three days the
Prince arrived at Derby. He was then within four or five
days' march of London, and had not yet encountered
a royal soldier. But he was not destined to get any
further. The same night (December 4th) the Prince's
council of war decided to commence the retreat on the
morrow. The grounds of this resolve were that the royal
army, under the Duke of Cumberland, was now believed
to be near, while the nearest reinforcements Prince Charles
Edward could count upon were in Scotland. The retreat
commenced; and the Manchester Regiment, more dispirited
thereby than the Scottish clans, began to lose many of its
men by desertion. The rebels were back in Manchester
by December 9th; and on the 12th, at nine o'clock in the
morning, after a night march, arrived at Preston. The
day after, General Oglethorpe, who had ridden with his
dragoons from Doncaster in three days, entered Preston.
It was the design of General Oglethorpe to overtake the
rebels on the Ribble; but having failed by a few hours
in the attempt to intercept the insurgents at this point,
Oglethorpe rested his dragoons at Preston a short time.
Prince Charles, however, did not loiter. Within six days
from leaving Preston his troops had gained Carlisle,
which was entered on the morning of December 19th.
The Scottish regiments had kept intact; but the men
of the Manchester regiment, foreseeing expatriation
even if they avoided capture, had deserted in numbers
while marching past their homes in Lancashire, and

on reaching Carlisle it was found that Colonel Towneley's command had been reduced by desertions from 300 to 114 men. An unfortunate decision to leave a garrison in Carlisle was taken by the Prince and his generals. Colonel Towneley and his Lancashire men, with 274 Scotsmen, were left in Carlisle to hold it as long as they could, and then, as was inevitable, to capitulate to the Duke of Cumberland, a ruthless enemy. To Colonel Towneley was given the command of the city itself, and Colonel Hamilton and his Scots held the castle. Prince Charles quitted Carlisle on the 20th of December; 'after having thanked the garrison for their devoted loyalty, and promised to relieve them as soon as he could.' Left at this perilous post, Colonel Towneley displayed a soldierly activity. He ordered cannon to be mounted on the walls, and *chevaux de frise* to be planted outside the city gates, to retard the enemy's approach. He sent out a party of his men to secure sheep for the food of the garrison, and himself stood sentinel on the wall, pistol in hand, ready to give his foragers the signal to return in the event of the appearance of the King's forces. To satisfy the claims for arrears of pay by his regiment, the Colonel headed a subscription among the officers with a contribution of £80. The day after the departure of Charles Edward Stuart, Cumberland's army appeared before Carlisle. After a week's investment, the Royal general commenced more active operations on December 28th, having procured a battery of cannon from Whitehaven. His shot soon began to tell upon the weak defences. Colonel Hamilton now suggested capitulation; but Colonel Towneley scouted the proposal. The Lancashire men of the garrison still shared the resolution of their Colonel to hold out. An officer of the regiment, Adjutant Syddall, who was eventually convicted of treason, and executed, before his death wrote a statement in which, referring to the surrender at Carlisle, he says:—'It was the opinion of every one in the garrison who had been in foreign service, that the place was tenable many

days, and, as the Elector's troops then lying before the town
were in bad condition, it is highly probable that a gallant
defence, which I strenuously insisted upon, would have
procured us such terms as to have prevented the fate to
which we were consigned.' But Governor Hamilton was
bent on surrender, and on the 30th December hoisted a
white flag on the castle in token of his desire to cease hos-
tilities. The Duke of Cumberland thereupon ceased firing.
Colonel Towneley then gave up the resistance, saying that
he and his Englishmen could do nothing after the Scots had
yielded up the castle. Captain Vere, a captured Royalist,
was sent with proposed terms of capitulation. The Duke's
reply was :—'All the terms His Royal Highness will or can
grant to the rebel garrison of Carlisle are, that they shall
not be put to the sword, but be reserved for the King's
pleasure.' The terms were accepted, and the castle and
city were occupied by the victors. The 'Manchester
Regiment,' when it surrendered, consisted of its colonel
(Towneley), six captains, six lieutenants, six ensigns ;
adjutant, chaplain, and quartermaster ; and no more than
ninety-three non-commissioned officers and privates. The
commissioned officers of the regiment were sent in waggons,
under a strong guard, to London. They were conducted
through the streets of the capital amid the coarse insults of
the populace, who had been influenced by representations
of the ferocious intentions of the Jacobites had they been
successful. The captives were lodged in the cells of
Newgate. All the officers were induced to expect that,
as they had served under French commissions, they
would be deemed prisoners of war, and would be
regularly exchanged. The name of Colonel Towneley was
inserted at the head of the list demanded by cartel from
France. The conduct of the prisoners during their confine-
ment was various. Colonel Towneley, for some reason or
other, had no relish for the society of his late companions
in the campaign, and showed much hauteur. He conversed

with no one but Mr. Saunderson, his Roman Catholic priest
and confessor.

"The trial of Francis Towneley for high treason took
place at the Court House of St. Margaret's Hill, Southwark,
on the 5th of July, 1746, before Lord Chief Justice Lee,
Lord Chief Justice Willes; Justices Wright, Dennison,
Foster, Abney; Barons Reynolds and Clive; with Sir
Thomas de Veil, Knt., and Peter Theobalds, Esq. (Justices
of the Peace for the county of Surrey, and gentlemen named
in the Special Commission). The counsel for the King were,
the Attorney-General; Sir John Strong; the Solicitor-
General; Sir Richard Lloyd; and the Hon. Mr. York.
The counsel for the prisoner were Mr. Sergeant Wynne
and Mr. Clayton. On the jury panel being called over,
several names were challenged by prisoner's counsel, but
at last a jury of twelve was sworn. The indictment, as
read by the Clerk of Arraigns, charged Francis Towneley,
late of the city of Carlisle, gentleman (Mr. Towneley was
only styled 'of Carlisle' because it was there he was
taken in arms against the King), and others named, with
having, at the city of Carlisle, 'falsely and traitorously
joined themselves together against their Lord and King,'
and 'waged and levied a public and civil war' against the
King, and so forth. To this indictment the prisoner
pleaded not guilty.—The Attorney-General (Sir Dudley
Rider) opened the case for the Crown. He undertook
to prove by evidence that 'the prisoner, with two others
whose names were Blood and Fletcher, and others their
confederates, did assemble in a warlike manner, and procured arms,' &c.; and 'composed a regiment for the
service of the Pretender to these realms,' &c.; and 'did
march through and invade several parts of this kingdom,
and unlawfully did seize his Majesty's treasure in many
places for the service of their villainous cause,' &c.;
and that, during the march, 'the prisoner, with other
rebels, in open defiance of his Majesty's undoubted

right and title to the crown of these realms, frequently
caused the Pretender's son to be proclaimed in a publick
and solemn manner as regent of these realms; and
himself marched at the head of a pretended regiment, which
they called the Manchester Regiment.' Sir John Strong,
for the prosecution, recounted that after the rebellion
headed by the Pretender's son had 'burrowed into England,'
the prisoner 'was with them in Lancashire, particularly at
Preston, and several other places, and then they proceeded
to Manchester, where the prisoner formed a regiment, and
accepted a commission to be colonel of the said regiment
from the eldest son of the Pretender, and wore a white
cockade, and a plaid sash, as a mark of his authority, and
the party he sided with; and then advanced from Manchester to Derby with his regiment, where the rebel army
halted some few days; but being apprehensive of the Duke
of Cumberland's attacking them, it so alarmed them, that
they marched back with great precipitation 'till they came
to Carlisle, where he acted as commandant of the city, and
gave out orders to the garrison, amongst which he ordered
the houses of some of his Majesty's faithful subjects to be
set on fire, but was afterwards obliged by the Duke to surrender to the King's pleasure. And,' added the learned
counsel, turning to the jury, 'though humanity may induce
you to have compassion towards the prisoner, yet if it is
proved that he is guilty of the crimes laid to him, the justice
of the nation calls aloud for his punishment.'—The Solicitor-
General (Hon. W. Murray, Esq.) proceeded to call witnesses.
The first witness, Roger Macdonald, swore that he knew
Colonel Towneley the prisoner, whom he saw at Derby;
and that on the retreat of the rebel army from thence,
prisoner marched at the head of the Manchester Regiment,
as its colonel; that he saw Mr. Towneley with a white
cockade in his hat, and a brace of pistols; and he was
accounted a principal officer between Lancaster and Preston;
and appeared at the head of the regiment, with colours fly-

ing, and drums beating, and that he had a plaid sash ; that
the Manchester Regiment had a flag with the words on one
side, 'Liberty and Property'; and, on the other, 'Church
and King'; and that the rebel army, on its march south-
ward, numbered 5,600 men, but not all armed. In cross-
examination, the witness admitted that he had been a rebel
soldier, and was expecting a pardon for his evidence. He
also stated that he saw Colonel Towneley during the retreat
from Derby on horseback very often, riding at the head of
his regiment on a bay horse.— Samuel Maddox, who had
been an ensign in the Manchester Regiment, swore he had
seen the prisoner at Manchester, in December, 1745 ; that
he was colonel of the Manchester Regiment ; in proof of
which he had seen a guard of that regiment mounted every
day, and sentinels placed at the prisoner's quarters ; that he
(witness) had carried colours, as ensign in the regiment, but
had no commission. Witness further deposed — that the
prisoner ordered the Manchester Regiment to be drawn up
in the church-yard in Manchester, where the Pretender's son
reviewed them ; that he marched at the head of the regiment
as colonel to Derby ; that the first day's march was from
Manchester to Wilmslow, where the prisoner appeared at
the head of his regiment with the white cockade in his hat,
plaid sash, brace of pistols, and a sword ; that witness had
been inclined to quit the regiment at Macclesfield, but dared
not do so on being told that if he did he would have his
brains knocked out; that when they were at Derby with
the rebel army, they beat up volunteers for the Manchester
Regiment, commanded by the Hon. Colonel Francis
Towneley, and the same was done by the particular order
and direction of the prisoner ; that when the rebel army
retreated from Derby, Colonel Towneley, the prisoner, and
some of his regiment, took out of a house between Derby
and Ashborn, a sack full of arms, which were concealed
under some old writings ; that the said arms were taken
with them to Ashborn, and lodged all night in the prisoner's

own room, and disposed of afterwards among his men;
that the prisoner had two sentinels always at his door
all night, for fear the Duke of Cumberland was nearer
them than they imagined; that when, on the retreat, they
came to Carlisle, the prisoner was made by the Pretender's son commandant of Carlisle, and had another
commission given him to raise a regiment of horse; that
as soon as the main body of the rebel army were
gone from Carlisle for Scotland, the prisoner took command of the whole rebel force left there, and that he
gave orders for the guns to be mounted, and also ordered
a house to be burnt, which was accordingly done, al-
leging that several of the King's forces had fired from
it, and annoyed the Pretender's army; that he particularly
directed several _chevaux de frise_ to be made, and fixed at
the gates and entrance to the city, to prevent his Majesty's
horse and dragoons from approaching it; further, that he
paid the men of his own company himself, and he heard
prisoner complain that he was fourscore pounds out of
pocket by paying his men; that before the capitulation,
witness heard the prisoner have some words, seemingly in
a great passion, with Colonel Hamilton, who was governor
of the Castle or Citadel of Carlisle, for surrendering the
place, and not making a defence to the last, and that he
heard the prisoner declare, that '_It was better to die by the
sword, than to fall into the hands of those damned
Hanoverians;_' also that he had seen him encouraging the
rebel soldiers to make sallies out on the King's forces.
Being cross-examined, Maddox said that though he had not
been promised a free pardon, he should be very thankful
to have a pardon. There were some other witnesses for the
prosecution, who gave similar evidence. The prisoner's
counsel opened his case for the defence with an account of
Francis Towneley's life before the events of the Rebellion.
The sole plea upon which the defence relied was that Colonel
Towneley held a French, not an English commission, and

was therefore entitled to be treated as a foreign prisoner of war. The prisoner's counsel said, after stating the prisoner's antecedents :— 'Thus it appears that he has been sixteen years in the service of France ; that he has had the French King's commission during all that time ; and consequently was as much in the service of France as any officer in the French army ; and therefore we are humbly of opinion, that Colonel Towneley has as just a right to the cartel as any French officer that has been taken by the English during the progress of the war between the two Kingdoms.' A minor plea was that the indictment was insufficient, for that it did not mention the day when the treason was done, as required by statute of 7th William III. Captain Carpenter, for the defence, was to prove that Colonel Towneley had served in the French army, held the French King's commission, and was supplied from France since his capture. But this plea was summarily set aside, on the ground that Mr. Towneley being a native of England and a subject of the English Crown, was forbidden to serve a Prince at war with England ; and General Carpenter was not suffered to give his evidence. John Heywood and Thomas Dickinson, both Manchester men, were called to impugn the evidence of the witness Maddox by representing the notorious badness of his character in Manchester. The Solicitor-General replied, showing that the indictment was not imperfect ; upon which the objection taken by prisoner's counsel was overruled by the court. Lord Chief Justice Lee summed up the evidence, and then the jury returned a verdict of 'guilty.' The Judges' warrant was sent to the Sheriff, and the sentence upon Francis Towneley and sixteen other prisoners, convicted at the same assize of the crime of high treason, was set forth according to the shocking formulæ then prescribed by English law in the execution of traitors :—' Let the several prisoners above-named return to the gaol of the county of Surrey from whence they came and from thence they must

d

be drawn to the place of execution and when they come
there they must be severally hanged by the neck but not
till they be dead for they must be cut down alive then
their bowels must be taken out and burnt before their
faces then their heads must be severed from their bodies
and their bodies severally divided into four quarters and
these must be at the King's disposal.' Of the seventeen
state prisoners eight were reprieved, and the other nine
were duly executed, among whom was Francis Towneley,
who was regarded as the most influential of the English
rebels. The accounts of the deportment of Mr. Towneley,
in the interval between his condemnation and his death,
and on the scaffold, concur in stating that his firmness was
unflinching, and his bearing heroic to the last. ' His
behaviour from the first of his being taken prisoner
at Carlisle to the time of his trial was of a piece ; he
frequently saying that he could not be hurt, for that he
had a commission from the King of France, and so
must be exchanged upon the cartel ; but when he was
convicted he seemed a little more serious, and often said
he expected no mercy. He was much more reserved than
many of his fellow-sufferers, and would not talk a great
deal to anybody but his particular friends and brother-
prisoners. The morning of his execution, and even
at the fatal place, he showed no manner of signs of dread,
but said he hoped he should be happy in the next world.'
The day of execution was Wednesday, July 30th, 1746 ; the
place was Kennington Common. The barbarous sentence
was carried out in each case in every particular. Mr.
Towneley and the other prisoners were simultaneously
hung, and while hanging were stripped naked by the sol-
diery ; but the hanging was the tamest feature in the tragedy. After Mr. Towneley had hung six minutes, he was
cut down, and having life in his body still, as it lay upon
the block to be quartered the executioner struck it several
blows on the breast, and this also failing to extinguish the

last ember of vitality, he cut the throat; he next proceeded to decapitate the body, which was then laid open, and the bowels and heart taken out and thrown into the fire, which soon consumed them. 'Then he slashed the four quarters, and put them with the head into a coffin, and they were carried to the New Jayl in Southwark, where they were deposited till Saturday, August 2nd.' The bodies were then buried, and the heads of several of the rebels were fixed on Temple Bar. Some authorities assert that the head of Mr. Towneley was among those exposed on the Bar, but this is now said to be a mistake. His body was given to an undertaker at Pancras, in London, by whom it was decently interred ; and the government, yielding to the application of the deceased gentleman's relatives, allowed them to have possession of the head. This relic is still preserved. A statement in *Notes and Queries* for December 7th, 1872, is to the effect that the head of Colonel Francis Towneley 'is now in a box in the library at 12 Charles Street, Berkeley Square, the residence of the present Col. Charles Towneley.' Thus perished a soldier and a gentleman whose unflinching courage, active and passive, in the cause he took up, extorts our sympathy and respect."

9. *Verses occasioned by the late Thanksgiving day*, p. 89. I have at least two published sermons preached in Boston, Mass., in grateful celebration of Culloden. The colony was most ignobly "loyal"—then.

10. *Epitaph on Queen Caroline Consort to George 2nd.* Earl Stanhope (in his *History*) states that he had long and diligently sought for these lines—in vain. There are other proofs that, when roused, the ordinarily languid Chesterfield, the writer of this Epitaph, could speak and write with no lack of force.

11. *Declaration*, p. 130. This historically important document was doubtless printed, more or less fully, at the time ; but our *MS.* supplies what bears on the face of it to be an authentic text. Both it and the succeeding

"Letter" to the Archbishop of York strongly tempt to
a commentary; but my space is more than exhausted
already.

And so I put these English Jacobite Ballads, &c., into
thy hands, gentle Reader, and leave thee to study them
in the light of saintly George Herbert's words :—"They
say it is an ill mason that refuseth any stone ; and there
is no knowledge but in a skilful hand serves, either posi-
tively as it is, or else to illustrate some other knowledge."
(*Remains.*)

ALEXANDER B. GROSART.

ENGLISH JACOBITE BALLADS, SONGS AND SATIRES.

A Song. Tune—Holloway House.

Oh! how shall I venture, or dare to reveal,
Too great for expressing, too good to conceal;
The Graces and Virtues that illustriously shine,
In the Prince that's descended from the Stuart's great line.

Oh! could I extoll as I love the dear Name,
And Suit my low Strains to my prince's high fame;
In Verses immortal his Glory should live,
And Ages unborn his merits survive.

But oh! thou great Heroe just Heir to the C.... n,
The World in amazement admires thy renown;
Thy Princely behaviour sets forth thy just praise,
In Trophies more lasting than Poets can raise.

Thy Valour in War, thy deportment in peace,
Shall be sung & admired when Divisions shall cease;
Thy foes in confusion shall yield to thy sway,
And those who now rule be compelled to obey.

A Song.

From Caledonia's loyal lands,
When justice uncontrouled commands,
The loyal clans in honour's cause,
Guarded by truth . . . .
Came to retrieve our antient laws.

B

A Song.

With royall Charles Minerva's Pride,
They came with Freedom Hand in hand,
And over the Hills and far away.

2.

To baulk their force and Stop their way,
Duke Billy's sent to die or Stray,
Whilst M. Wade 'midst all his Schemes,
Sleeping . . of conquest only dreams ;
The Bishops too with reverend looks,
Turn red coats now and damn their books ;
Laun sleeves laid by, their prayers forgot,
And all their cry's a Popish plott ;
Over the Hills, &c.

3.

Britons be firm in Britains cause,
Assert your right, suport your laws ;
Defend the truth, Great Charles obey,
And Usurpation drive away ;
Then Sons of War with martial flame,
You'll bravely merit lasting fame,
Great Charles will Britains scepter sway,
And Hanoverians rue the Day,
Over the Hills and far away.

The 5th Ode of the 4th Book of Horace immitated.

Ode.

O Prince from English Princes Sprung,
Why does thou stay from us so long ;
Thy Absence, James, thy Subjects mourn,
And longing sigh for thy return.

Thou only canst our Spirits Chear,
We can't be gay till thou art here,
Till thou are here & like the Spring,
Givest a new life to every thing.

As a fond Mother makes her moan,
Incessant for her only Son,
Whom the cross winds & Stormy main,
Beyond the promised year detain.

Pensive she dwells upon the Shore,
With Tears his safety to implore ;
So with eager fond desire,
Britons their lawful King require.

Our Envious neighbours puff'd with pride,
May now with ease our Scheemes deride,
And scoffingly rejoice when told,
Our Senates bribed & places Sold.

Blessed with thy mild and equal reign,

We shall our freedom boast again,
Opprcsive Armies shall not stand,
Nor Alien Fools devour our Land.

United in thy righteous Cause,
We shall impose on Europe Laws,
The Belgian Brutcs shall homage pay,
And own our Title to the Sea.

Justice that long from us is fled,
Shall rcar again her Lawful Head ;
All party rage & frauds shall cease,
All shall be harmony & peace.

Fly speedy then & succour bring,
Too long we've borne the foreign King,
'Tis time t' enjoy our rights & thee,
From fetters & from Taxes free.

What e'er we do, what e'er we are,
to Heavcn we dayly send this prayer,
" Restore our Monarch to his throne,
" And send these Booby Germans home.

Written in 1747.   A Song.

As the Devil was walking our Britain's fair Isle,
George Spy'd in his face a particular smile,
And said, My old freind, if you've Leizure to Tarry
Let's have an Account of what makes you so merry.

Derry &c.

Old Belzebub turned at a voice he well knew,
And Stoping cry'd oh ! Brother George is it you,
Were my business of consequence ever So great,
I always find time on my friends for to wait.   Derry, &c.

This morning at seven I set out from Rome,
Most fully intending eer this to have been home ;
Pray stay Sir, says George, & took hold of his hand,
you know St. James's is at your Command.

Pray what says old James, our great monarch begun,
And what does he think of his brave gallant Son ;
Why when first I beheld him, old Satan reply'd,
He seemed to have very great hopes of his Side.

But soon from the North there arrived an Express,
With papers that gave me great joy I confess,
Defeated was Charles & his forces all gone,
I thought on my Soul I should leap o'er the moon.

Of Great Charles's descendants I am only afraid,
Against my Dominions their projects are laid,
Leave a Stuart to govern Old England again,
Religion and Honesty then too might reign.

I often trip over to France and to Spain,
To visit my Princes and see how they reign,

But of all my good Servants North, East, South & West,
I speak it sincerely George thou are the best.

George pleased with the Compliment, smiled like a fool
And bowing said Sir I hope you dont flatter your Tool,
Tho' the trouble I give you is not much I must own,
For as to religion you know I have none.

Then as to my Offspring there's Freddy my Son,
Whom you wish & I wish may come to the throne,
for by all men of Wisdom & Sense 'tis allowed,
If he does there no harm, he will do there no good.

Then there's Billy my Darling and Blood thirsty Boy,
He'll ravish, and plunder, burn, kill & destroy,
I need say no more for you know very well ;
That Murder's a virtue in which he excells.

They shook hands at parting and both bid adieu,
Old Belzebub muttered these words as he flew,
May Thee & thy race for ever reign on,
For the Devil can't find such a race when you've gone.

Nero the Second.

Monstrum Horrendum.

As Nero Laughing saw the flames consume,
The worlds Metropolis Imperial Rome ;

So George unpitying greived & Senseless sneercd,
When England's Capital in flames appeared ;
Nor is the paralell to them confined,
If we compare their guilt of every kind ;
Nero possessed Britannicus's Crown,
George has usurped our royal James's throne ;
Nero with thundering Edicts first began,
To try the terrors of his brutal reign ;
George by his furious proclamations shews,
A Spirit prone to rage, averse to Laws ;
Nero in masks & revels spent the night,
George for the business of the throne unfit,
In Plays & Balls and Junkets does delight :
Nero with Horror of his crimes grew mad,
Scar'd by the Ghosts of those whose Blood he shed :
George conscious of his murders, gloomy sits,
Worn out with spleen & Hippocondriac fits ;
Not all his feasts can drown his inward care,
For murdered Loyalists are present there ;
Such is our George & such we find his court,
Where royal Ideots with their train resort ;
Where William struts with patriot Blood besmear'd,
Where Bullies swarm, & ruffians are preferred ;
Where Atheists, Turks, and Bawds the Throne surround ;

And a strange monster (Ministry) compound ;
Oh free Born Britons, since a Tyrant reigns,
Assert your Liberty, shake off your Chains ;
Let us in justice rival antient Rome,
Let Nero's' vices meet with Nero's doom,
And then call James your King from Exile home.

A Speech

Made by Arthur Lord Balmerino at the Barre of the house
of Lords Aug : 18. 1746.

My Lords

It is Natural for a man when his life is
in doubt, to catch at any the last possibility of saving himself ; .. with this view I disputed the Indictement brought
against me, & this was the whole of my defence: I made
no attempt to disapprove the facts alledged in it, I neither
can, nor will deny them . . . . This hazardous Undertaking, My Lords, was not entered upon rashly, nor
inadvisedly: the principles on which I acted, I thought
just and Honest ; and tho' my notions should be mistaken,
yet as my actions have been agreable to the dictates
of my own conscience, I have hopes I shall not be
unpardonable in the sight of God ; . . . . But, My Lords,

should my opinion be well grounded, then I have nothing to fear, but from your Lordships Sentence ; and I trust in God, I shall meet it, as becomes a Man.

It would, my Lords, be indecent for me, in this place, to say more in Vindication of myself, least I should seem to reflect on the principles your Lordships profess, which, my Lords, is far from my intention, for I would not re-reproach any man because his sentiments differ from mine.

I have been the occasion of much trouble to your Lordships, for which I entreat your Lordships to pardon me ; Farther Have I nothing to ask : If I find mercy It shall be wellcome, If not I shall submit myself with patience to the penalties of your Laws.

.

Arthurus Dominus de Balmerino Decollatus 19th Augt 1746 Ætatis 55. By a Lady.

Here is the man to Scotland ever dear
Whose honest Heart ne'er felt a guilty fear,
By Principles, not mean self interest sway'd,
The Victor left to bring the vanquish'd aid.
His courage manly, but his words were few,
Content in Poverty and owned it too ;

C

In life's last scene with dignity appears,
Not for himself, but for his country fears :
Pities the Graceful partner of his fall,
And nobly wishes he might die for all :
Ev'n Enemies convinced, his worth approved,
He fell admired, Lamented, and Beloved.

Vers sur le Prince Edoüard.

Peuples jadis sy fier, aujourdhy sy servile,
Des princes malheureux vous n'estes plus l'asyle ;
Vos enemies vaincus aux Champs de Fontenoy,
A leur propres vainqueurs ont imposé la loy,
Et cette indigne paix qu 'Aragon vous procure,
Est pour eux un triomphe, et pour vous une injure,
Helas! auriez vous courû tant d'Hazards,
Pour placer une Femme au trône des Cœsars,
Pour voir l'heureux Anglois dominateur de l'onde,
Vorturer dans ses ports tout l'or du Nouveau Monde ;
Et le Fils de Stuart par vous mêmes appellé,
Aux frayeurs de Brunswick lâchement immolé,
Et toy que les Flatteurs ont paré d'un vain titre,
De l'Europe en ce jour te diras tu l'arbitre ?
Lorsque dans tes Etats tu ne peut conserver,

Un Heros que le Sort n'est pas las d'eprouver ;
Mais qui dans les Horreurs d'une vie agitée,
Au Sein de l'Angleterre, à sa perte exilé ;
Abandonnée des Siens, fugitif, mis a prix,
Se vit toujours du moins plus libre qu' à Paris.
De l'amitié des roys Exemple memorable,
Et de leurs interests victime deplorable ;
Tu triomphe, Cher Prince, au milieu de tes fers,
Sur Toy dans les moments tous les yeux sont ouverts,
Un peuple genereux est jugé du merite,
Va, revoquer l'arrêt d'une race proscrite,
Tes Malheurs ont changés les esprits prevenus,
Dans la Cour des Anglois tous tes droits sont connus,
Plus sures & plus flatteurs que ceux de la Naissance
Ces droits vont doublement affermir ta puissance,
Mais sur le trône assis, cher Prince, souviens toy
Que ce peuple Superbe est jaloux de sa loy,
N'a jamais honoré du titre de grand Homme,
Un lache Complaisant des Francois et de Rome.

Quel est le triste Sort des malheureux François,
Reduits à s'affliger dans les bras de la Paix,

Plus heureux et plus grands au milieu des alarmes,
Ils repandoient leurs Sangs, mais sans verser des larmes ;
Qu'on ne veux vante plus les charmes du repos,
Nous aimons mieux courir à des perils nouveaux ;
Et vainqueurs avec gloire, ou vaincu sans foiblesses,
N'avoir point à pleurer de honteuses bassesses :
Edouard fugitif a laissé dans nos cœurs
Le desespoir honteux d'avoir etés vainqueurs
A quoi nous servoit-il d'enchainer la Victoire,
Avec moins de Lauriers nous avions plus de gloire,
Et contraint de ceder à la loy du plus fort,
Nous aurions pu du moins en accuser le Sort ;
Mais trahir Edoüard lorsque l'ou peut combattre,
Immoler à Brunswick le Sang de Henry Quartre ;
Et de George vaincu subir les dures loix.
O François . . . O Louis . . . . . O protecteurs rois !
Est-ce pour les trahir qu'on porte ce vain titre ?
Est-ce en les trahissant qu'on devient leur arbitre ?
    Un roy qui d'un Heros se declare l'appuy ;
Doit l'elever au throne, ou tomber avec luy ;
Ainsy pensoient les rois que celebre l'histoire,
Ainsy parloient tous ceux à qui parloit la gloire ;
Et qu' auroient ils pensés ces Monarques fameux
S'ils avoient pu prevoir qu'un roy plus puissant qu'eux,

Appellant un Heros au secours de la France
Contractant avec luy la plus sainte alliance,
L'exposeroient sans force, au plus affreux hazards,
Du fureur de la mer, des saisons & de Mars ?
Et qu'ensuite unissant la foïblesse au parjure,
Ils oubliroient sermens, gloire, Sang et Nature,
Et servant de Brunswick le Sistéme cruele,
Traineroient enchaineè cet Heros à l'autel ?
Brunswick! te faut-il donc de sy grandes victimes
Et pour avoir la paix .. Louis .. faut'il des crimes ?
Quoy Biron .... votre roy vous l'a-t-il ordonnée,
Edoüard ... est ce vous d' huissiers environnée ?
Estes vous de Henry ce fils digne de l'etre ?
Sans doute à vos malheurs j'ay du vous reconnoître ;
Mais je vous reconnois bien plus à vos vertus,
O Louis .. vos sujets de douleurs abattus,
Respectent Edoüard captif et sans couronne,
Il est roy dans les fers qu'êtes vous sur le trône,
J'ay vu tomber le Sceptre au pieds de Pompadour,
Mais fut'il relevé par les mains de l'amour ?
Belle Agnes tu n'est plus ! Le fier Anglois vous domte
Tandis que Louis dort dans le Sein de la honte ;
Et d'une femme obscure indignement epris
Il oublie en ses bras nos pleurs et nos mepris ;

Belle Agnes, tu n'est plus ! ton altière tendresse,
Dedaigneroit un roy fletrit par la foiblesse ;
Tu pouvois reparer les malheurs d'Edoüard,
En offrant ton amour à ce brave Stuart :
Helas ! pour t'imiter il faut de la Noblesse
Dans ces lieux tout est vil, ministre & maitresse,
Tous disant à Loüis qu'il agit en vray roy
Du bonheur des François qu'il se fait une loy ;
Qu'il vent et cherche en tout le Salut de la France,
Voila la flatterie ! . . . . et voici la prudence !
Peut on par l'infamie arriver au bonheur,
Un peuple s'affoiblit par le seul deshonneur ;
Rome cent fois vaincu en devenoit plus fière
Et ses malheurs plus grands la rendoit plus altière,
Ainsy Rome parvient à dompter l'univers,
Mais Toy lache ministre, ignorant ou pervers
Tu trahis ta patrie, et tu la deshonore,
Tu poursuis un Heros que l'univers adore,
Ou diroient que Brunswick t'a transmis ses fureurs
Que Ministre inquiet des ses justes terreurs,
Le nom seul d'Edouard t'epouvante et te gêne,
Mais apprend quel sera le puit de cette haine,
Albion sent enfin qu' Edouard est son roy
Digne par ses vertus de lui donner la loy.

Elle offre sur le trône asyle à ce grand homme
Trahi tout à la fois par la France & par Rome,
Et bientôt les François tremblans, humiliées,
D'un nouvel Edouard viendront baiser les pieds,
Voila les tristes fruits d'un Olivier funeste
Et de nos vains lauriers le deplorable reste.

The Accomplished Hero,
Or Caledonian Songstress.

On the green borders of the Silver Tweed,
Whose quiv'ring current parts the flow'ry mead,
There stands a venerable shady grove,
Which PAN delights in & the Muses love ;
Where from their Urns, three lovely NAIDS pour,
A clear cascade, whose rushing waters roar ;
Spreading with lucid rills the vales below,
To make ten thousand flowers spring & grow ;
Here have the muses bath'd as poets Sing,
There trod the Velvet margent of the Spring ;
No boisterous wind presumes to press these trees,
They only are caressed by Zephyrs breeze.
Here too the Nymphs & Fawns oft take delight,
To spend in Sportive dance the Jovial Night :

Whilst Pan with rural pipe soft music plays
(Accordant Measures to harmonious Lays)
Nor the Moon by Night, nor the Sun by Day,
Pierce thro' the gloom, with his most active ray,
Th' embow'ring foliage darkens so complete,
So close the interwove Espaliers meet ;
Silence and shade, and Gales refreshing play
Thro' this sequestered scene both night and Day ;
Hid by the trembling leaves, and Philomel,
Does in Melodious Strains, her sorrow tell,
Pained by the thorn her bosom's wo'nt to press
And wails her ancient woes without redress :

 Hard by, the Linnet with delightfull note ;
Pours forth the musick of her warbling throat ;
And to the Swains with her sweet Songs does bring,
The welcome Tidings of approaching Spring,
That Philomela's self is jealous grown,
Of Sounds so soft, so equal to her own :

 One day they spy'd a YOUTH of lovely mein,
Who never in the grove till then was Seen ;
Tall was his Stature, amiable his face,
Majestic, Noble, and of manly grace ;
Him Harmony does for her patron chuse,

And every Art, and every gentle Muse.
First when they viewed him with admiring Eyes
They took him for Appollo in disguise ;
Hiding his radiant and Ambrosial Locks,
As when he tended King Admetus flocks ;
He from celestial Lineage secmed to Spring,
A youthful HERO, or at least a KING.
The feathered Choristers with rage divine,
Inspired at once by all the Tuneful nine,
With sounds adapted to immortal Lays,
In Concert they began to Sing his praise :
    Who is this SHEPHERD PRINCE? this God unknown,
Are we not his ? and is he not our own ?
Whose royal presence thus adorns this place,
He's heavenly born, and not of mortal race ;
With gentle Courtesy he wins our Hearts ;
pleased with our Songs, he cherishes the Arts ;
Science he loves, and poetry is his Care,
And mercy fills his Soul beyond Compare.
The GRACES all, and all'the VIRTUES wait,
To render him as Amiable as Great.
    Now when the raptured Song was warmer grown
The Nightingale pursued the Theme alone.

Guard him Ye Gods, protect him more and more,
Shower on him blessings from your endless Store ;
Give him in every Virtue to encrease,
To live a Conqueror, and to die in peace ;
To flourish, thrive, and bloom as he begun,
As the Gay flower that opens to the Sun ;
May this Young HERO every wish Complete,
May his delights be rational and Sweet ;
May his renown both far and near be Sung,
May all the GRACES hang upon his Tongue ;
May JOVE'S fair Daughter her rare Gifts impart,
And all MINERVA'S wisdom fill his Heart.

The LINNET here with vocal ardour vy'd,
Resumed the Arduous Strain and thus replyed.

His Voice with such persuasive Sounds inspire,
As ORPHEUS could not equal with his lyre,
Wait on him VICTORY till he exceeds,
In Godlike Actions and Heroic deeds,
Great HERCULES ; Let him undaunted be
As fierce ARCHILLES, and from wounds as free ;
Daring as HOMER does of him rehearse,
But make him not so Savage nor so fierce,
But good and wise, beneficent and great,
Indulgent, Merciful, Compassionate.

Let worth and want in him a father find,
And let him be the Darling of Mankind ;
While the Chaste MUSES plant without controul,
The Seeds of every Virtue in his Soul.
  Again the Shrilling Notes the Songsters join,
Where all the power of voice and Skill combine.
  He loves our Songs, takes pleasure in our Art,
MUSICK has charms to win his tender Heart ;
It souths, it softens, lulls to pleasing rest,
Harmonious truths sink deep into his breast ;
As the cool dew refreshing solace yeilds,
To the sing'd Herbage of the Sun-burnt fields ;
And O YE GODS to whom he Stands allyed
In many virtues, taint him not with pride :
Grant him a loyal people to possess,
Crown all his days with fortune and success ;
Yeild Plenty's cornucopia to his hand,
And a new Golden Age to bless th' impov'rish'd land.
HIM nations shall with acclamations meet
And flowers spring and grow beneath his feet.
  All nature while they Sung, was hush'd as Death,
The flower-kissing Zephyrs, held their Breath ;
And every flower in the grove that grew,
Blush'd, bloomed, or blowed with variagated Hue :

The three pure fountains of impetuous force
Their rushing waters stopt, and stay'd their Course :
The SATYRS and the FAWNS that skip & bound,
Prick'd their sharp ears, & listn'd to the Sound :
ECHO alone (who can't her tongue refrain)
Told the Sweet Accents to the rocks again ;
Flocking together like a Swarm of Bees,
The DRYADS hasten from their hollow trees,
To Gaze with admiration and Surprise,
His praise their Ears, his person charms their Eyes ;
They view him and review him with amaze,
Their wonder still encreasing as they gaze,
Th' accomplished HERO to behold so young,
Whom PHILOMEL and her Companion Sung.

The Loyal Resolution.

Dear Royal Prince ! I'le ne'er repent,
　　What hitherto I have Spoken ;
My vows I made not with intent,
　　that they should e'er be broken ;
Antipathies shall well agree,
　　The Stars cleave to the Center
E'er I permit disloyalty,
　　Within my breast to enter.

The distant Poles shall both unite
  And drain the boundless Ocean,
Sol from his Chariot shall alight
  And Stop his rapid Motion :
The frame of Nature Shall dissolve,
  Forgetting time and Season ;
E'er Wiggish principles involve,
  My Soul in horrid Treason.

Usurping Nassau shall convince
  His German imitator ;
He'd better be a banished Prince,
  Than a Commanding Traytor,
Old Noll shall from the Shades descend,
  And teach the Wiggs obedience,
E'er I for George's race contend,
  Or forfeit my allegiance.

What Tho' these Sons of Baal combine,
  To load me with afflictions,
My hope is fix'd in power divine
  And not in vain Predictions.
My Cause is right, my God is just,
  He'll send me Consolation ;
And thro' his mercy still I trust,
  To see a RESTORATION.

The humble Address of the Tower of London to George yᵉ 2d 1748.

Let England now lament her freedom lost,
And think how dear a German king has cost,
Too late grown wise, let Tories think with tears,
How ill they've husbanded these threescore* years.
Just is my joy ! my transports are Sincere,
Thee GEORGE I welcome, Thee my walls revere ;
Thy German Savage rule proclaims my power,
And in bright terror reinstates the Tower :
No more shall gaping Wits, and Staring Clowns,
With aukard Jests deride my harmless Guns.
No longer shall my idle Axes rust,
Or massey chains lay useless in the dust ;
No more shall tender Damsells flock to see
My Lions, far less terrible than Thee ;
Their dens shall now be Stocked with human prey,
And Bones of MARTYRED NOBLES pave the way :
No Sex, no Rank, no Dignity or Age,
No Virtue shall appease or Stem your rage ;
Thus then my power no longer shall be Scorned,
But all my Spires with Patriots heads adorned,
My Hill shall be enriched with Loyal Blood,
And gazing mobs wade thro' the Crimson flood ;
Thus Thou and I shall rule this stubborn Land,
With Iron rod, and by the Sword Command.

* From yᵉ
revolution
1688

A Song.

Would you see three Nations bubled
  By a pious trick of State :
With our Taxes dayly doubled,
  Till we sink beneath the wcight?
Would you understand the reason,
  Why these woes we justly bear?
They're the due rewards of Treason,
  In which course we blindly Steer!

Would you see the Man of Sorrows,
  Then behold great JAMES the just,
Tho' Grief his cheeks hath plowed in furrows,
  Yet in him Still put your trust?
His Majesty's divinely sacred,
  Which your conscious hearts must own,
'Twas your blind misguided hatred,
  Drove him from his Lawful throne?

Think not but his tears are numbered,
  And his sorrows duly weighed,
Think with what ills we've been incumbered,
  Since God's laws we've disobeyed.
Would you be accounted Christians,
  And wipe off this fatal Stain,
Banish hence those vile Philistians,
  And call home your King again?

Peace and Plenty then ensuing,
  Halcyon days shall come again,
Heaven shall then repair your ruin,
  And drop fatness down in rain.
All nature in one voice consenting,
  Brittain's Joys shall then proclaim,
The vocal Hills and Vales exulting,
  Shall proclaim a STUART'S reign.

The Lamentation of DAVID over SAUL and JONATHAN Imitated.

1.

I mourn the Glory of our Isle,
  A Hero brave betray'd,
I mourn a land devote to Spoil,
  And horrid CARNAGE made.

2

How fell the mighty in the fight
  on that accursed Morn,
When from the Head which claimed its right,
  We saw the Laurels torn.

3.

Oh ! tell it not in Brunswick's street,
  Nor publish it in Zell ;   .
Least Stranger Maids in Songs repeat
  How Low the mighty fell ?

4.

Ye Grampian mountains ! on your Head,
  Nor dew descend, nor rain,

The Target there in vain was spread,
   The broad Sword drawn in vain!

5.

Alas! what need of kindly showers,
   Where DESOLATION reigns ;
The Sword and flames the land devours,
   And Scarce a Scot remains.

6.

For Lo! the bloody Welp like Death,
   At Cotts and Castles knocks,
Spares nothing that has human breath,
   Nay murders Herds and flocks.

7.

The SLAUGHTERED WARRIORS swell the Hills,
   Yet the relentless foe,
The Battle done, the wounded kills,
   No suppliant 'scapes the blow.

8.

Not So the Gallant PRINCE behaved,
   On Gladsmuir's luckier plain,
He fought, he conquered & he saved,
   Nor triumphed o'er the Slain.

9.

How lovely all his Acts! How bright,
   The books of Fame among!
More than Eagle swift in flight,
   More than a lion strong.

E

10.

Ye Maidens o'er your lovers weep,
　Fallen in a noble Cause,
The Harvest which they strove to reap,
　Was antient rights & LAWS!

11.

Ye Daughters of the Land lament,
　Your hope betrayed & sold!
He would have shone its ornament,
　And trimm'd your plaids with Gold!

12.

How on the Native Hills so high,
　The loyal Clans were beat!
And how, oh! Charles, when thou were't nigh,
　Could happen such defeat!

13.

For thee, I suffer great distress,
　For thee I wear my Sword,
My love for thee I can't express　.
　Thou art my LAWFUL LORD.

14.

My Love for Woman is far less,
　Oh! thou my Soul's desire,
With all the Stuart's tenderness,
　And Sobiesky's fire.

15.

Alas! how are the mighty slain,
　Their warlike weapons broke!
A race may soon arise again,
　And Burst this foreign yoke.

The Tears of Scotland.

Mourn! Hapless Caledonia! Mourn!
Thy Banished Prince and laurels torn!
Thy Sons for Valour long renowned
Lay slaughtered on their Native ground!
Thy Hospitable roofs no more,
Invite the Stranger to the door ;
In smoaking ruins sunk they lye,
The Monuments of CRUELTY!

2.

The Wretched owner sees afar,
How all becomes the prey of War ;
Bethinks him of his Babes & Wife,
Then smites his breast & curses life ;
Thy swains are famish'd on the rocks,
Where late they fed their wanton flocks!
Thy ravish'd Virgins shriek in vain,
Thy Infants perish on the plain!

3.

What boots it that in ev'ry clime,
Thro' the wide-Spreading waste of time,
Thy martial Glory crown'd with praise,
Still shone with undiminish'd blaze?
Thy tow'ring spirit now is broke,
Thy neck is bended to the Yoke ;
What foreign Arms could never quell,
By Civil rage and rancour fell.

4

The rural Pipe and merry lay,
No more shall cheer the happy day ;
No social Scenes of Gay delight,
Beguile the dreary winter Night ;
No strains but those of sorrow flow,
No sounds be heard but those of Woe ;
Whilst the pale Phantoms of the Slain,
Glide nightly o'er the silent plain !   ,

5.

O Baleful cause !   O fatal morn !
Accursed to Ages yet unborn !
The Sons against their Fathers stood,
And Parents shed their Children's Blood ;
Yet when the rage of Battle ceased,
The Victor's rage was not appeased ;
The Naked and Forlorn must feel,
Devouring flames & murdering Steel.

6.

The Pious Mother doomed to Death,
For refuge wanders o'er the Heath,
The bleak winds wistle round her head,
Her helpless Orphans cry for Bread ;
Bereaft of shelter, food, and Freinds,
She views the shades of night descend,
And stretch'd beneath th' inclement skies,
Weeps o'er her tender Babes and DIES.

7.

Whilst vital blood flows in my veins
And unimpaired remembrance reigns,
Resentment for my Country's fate
Within my filial breast shall beat,
And Spite of her insulting foe
My Sympathizing Verse shall flow;
Mourn! Hapless Caledonia Mourn!
Thy Banished PRINCE and LAURELS torn!

The Heroes.

Of all the Jobs that e'er were past
   Our house since time of Jobbing,
Sure none was ever like the last
   E'en in the days of Robin;
for he Himself had blush'd for shame,
   At this polluted Cluster,
Of fifteen Nobles of great fame,
   All bribed by one false muster.

Two Dukes*a* on Horseback first appear   *a*Montague
   Both tall and of great prowess,   & Bolton.
Two little Barons*b* in the rear   *b*Edge Cumbe
   (for they're you know the lowest)   & Herbert.
But high and low they all agreed
   To do whatever Man dared;

Those ne'er so tall as those that fall
A foot below the Standard.

Three regiments One Duke^c contents   ^cMontague.
With two more places you know
Since his Bath Knights his Grace delights
    In tria juncta in Uno.
Now, Bolton comes with beat of Drums,
    Tho' fighting be his Loathing,
He much dislikes, both Guns and pikes
    But relishes the Cloathing.

Next does advance defying France,
    A Peer in wonderous bustle,
With Sword in hand he Stout does stand,
    And brags his Name is Russel :
He'll beat the French from ev'ry trench
    And blow them off the Water ;
By Sea and land he does command
    And looks an arrant Otter.

But of all this clan there is neer a Man,
    for Bravery that can be,
(Tho' Ancaster should make a Stir)
    Compared with Marquis GRANBY ;
His Sword and dress both well express
    His Courage not exceeding,

And by his Hair you would almost swear
He's Valiant Charles of Sweden.

The next are Harcourt, Halifax,
  And Falmouth, Choice Commanders!
For these the Nation we must Tax,
  But ne'er send them to flanders :
Two Corps of Men do Still remain,
  Earl Cholmondeley's & Earl Berkley's,
The last I hold not quite so bold,
  As formerly was Herc'les.

And now Dear Gower, thou man of power,
  And Comprehensive Noddle,
Tho' you've the gout, yet as you are Stout,
  Why wa'nt you placed i' th' Saddle ;
Then you might ride to either Side,
  chuse which King you'd serve under,
But, Dear Dragoon, change not too Soon,
  For fear of the other Blunder.

This faithful Band shall ever Stand,
  Defend our faith's Defender,
And keep us free from Popery ;
  The French & the Pretender.
Now God bless all our Ministry,
  May they the Crown environ,

To hold in Chains whate'er Prince reigns
And rule with rods of Iron.

U D.

Famed were the Bards in old untainted days,
When only merit felt the breath of praise ;
When Heaven-born Muses taught the tuneful lay,
The brave to honour and the Good display ;
Virtue's fair form, tho' cloath'd in rags, to Sing
And loath the Baneful court and sinful King.

But now sad Change ! no more the Poets theme,
Tastes thy chaste waters, Hypocrene's Stream ;
His breast no more the sacred Sisters urge,
Of truth the patrons and of vice the Scourge :
Venal he seeks the Court and shuns the Lawn,
On Pride to flatter & on power to fawn,
Pours forth his incense at the Courtier's shrine,
To raise the royal race, to race divine :

He, who would toil in Honour's arduous track,
Must Virtue seek alone, for Virtue's sake,
For now, to Merit, are unwonted things,
The Breath of Poets and the smiles of Kings ;
See ! where the rhyming throng on William wait,
And patch up ev'ry worth to make him great ;
Sing how he triumph'd on fair Clifton's Green,

And how his mind is lovely as his mein ;
Call Antients, Heroes, from their Seats of Joy,
To see their fame outshadowed in a Boy ;
Rob ev'ry Urn and every page explore,
And tell how Cæsar's deeds, are deeds no more ;
No more shall guide the War, or fire the Song,
But WILLIAM be the theme of ev'ry Tongue,
Whilst BRUNSWICK *Kings Brittania's* throne shall grace,
And GEORGE'S Virtues live in George's race.
Such is the Theme the flatt'ring songsters chuse,
And oh ! how worthy of the theme the Muse.

Whilst lo ! a Youth arises in the North
Of royal Virtues and of royal Birth ;
With worth, which in the dawn of ages shewn,
Without the claim of Birth had gained a Crown ;
Tho' in him ev'ry grace and virtue joy[n]
To add new lustre to the STEWARTs line ;
Tho' Vict'ry makes the Youthful CHARLES his care,
No Bard attends on his triumphal Carr,
On firmer Base, he builds his Sure applause
Recouvered Freedom and protected LAWS.

Say, SCOTLAND, say, for you must surely know,
You felt the rupture, and you feel the Woe,
Say whilst he trod upon thy kindly Earth,
The Genial Soil that gave his father Birth ;

F

Did not his Outstreched hand with Bounty Spread
Paternal blessings on thy children's Head?
Hush them to peace, amidst the Din of War,
And still the Matron's Sigh & Virgin's fear?
Bid peaceful plenty wave upon thy plain,
The untouched harvest of the Golden Grain?
Did not thy Youth enlivened by his name,
Glow for the fight & ardent pant for fame?
Strove not each reverend Sage & Hoary Sire,
His worth to honour and his Sense admire?
Did not his form, with ev'ry beauty graced,
Raise a Chaste rapture in each Virgin's breast?

But when he quits the Scene of soft delight,
The graceful measure for the dreadful fight,
Say saw thy plains, when many a Deathless Name,
When BRUCE, when WALLICE, fought their way to fame,
When DOUGLAS race Heroic, nobly rose
Secured thy freedom, and repelled thy foes;
Said they e'er one among the chieftien throng,
So ripe in Glory, and in years so Young?
Whose pride, not more to vanquish than to save,
In conquest gentle, as in action Brave;
Like Philip's Son victorious o'er the Course,
With skill superior, and inferior force;
Like Zenophon secure 'midst hostile bands,
He led his glorious few from distant lands;

                                    And join to

And join to sense of head, the fire of heart,
Of one the courage, and of one the art.
Whilst Virtue lives, and Honour has a name,
Whilst deeds Heroic fill the rolls of Fame ;
First in the list shall Seaton have a place,
And FALKIRK plain, Mark HAWLEY, thy disgrace.

    Now change the Scene, and show the sad reverse,
Where Winter's blasts th' autumnal smiles disperse :
Where the fierce HANOVER directs the Storm,
And Hawley joys his mandates to perform ;
To whom compared an ALVA'S name is sweet,
Brave in the field tho' cruel in the State :
See thro' the land how hostile fury burns,
And peopled Vales to rueful desarts turns,
See how the smoaking Country round thee groans,
Invokes in vain the desolated Towns !
See Age unreverenc'd, draged from peaceful ease,
And linked in dreary Jails to loath'd disease !
Before their Sires see ravished, Maids complain,
And lift their beauteous eyes to Heaven in vain !
Oh ! more than Savage ! who pursue with rage,
The bloom of Beauty and the hoar of Age !
And what exploits exalt this Heroe's praise,
Whence spring these Laurels which the poets raise !

Spring they from conquests o'er the Village tame.
The Aged Sire, and the blooming Dame!

View well the Sketch, and say of which the face,
Presents the royal mark of SCOTLAND'S race?
He who would save thee from destruction's blast,
Or He who lays thy glories in the Dust?

So judged of old the Good King DAVID'S Heir,
With nice discernment the contending fair;
Repulsed the Dame who cruel would destroy,
And blessed the feeling Mother with her BOY.

Finis.

A Birth Day Ode.
On the 20th December, 1747.

A while forget the Scenes of woe,
Forbid a while the Tears to flow,
  The pitying Sighs to rise ;
Turn from the Ax the thoughts away,
'Tis CHARLES that bids us crown the day,
  And end the night in joys.

2.

So when black clouds & beating rain,
With Storms the face of nature stain,
  And all in gloom appears.
If Phœbus deigns a short-lived smile,
The face of Nature charms a while,
  A while the prospect chears.

3.

Come then & while we largely pour,
Libations to the genial Hour,
  That gave our Hero birth ;
Let us invoke the tuneful nine,
T' inspire a Theme like theirs divine,
  And Sing our Hero's worth.

4.

How on its tender infant years,
The careful Hand of Heaven appears,
  To watch its chosen care ?
Changed to ev'ry thing but truth,
Virtuous affliction, formed his Youth
  Instruction, tho Severe !

5.

No Sinful Court it's poison lent,
An early bane his life to taint,
    And blast it's young renown,
His father's virtues fired his heart,
His father's sufferings truths impart,
    That formed him for a throne.

6.

How at an age when pleasures charms,
Alure the Stripling to her Arms,
    He formed the great design ;
T' assert his injured father's Cause,
Restore his suff'ring country's laws,
    And prove his right divine.

7.

How when on Scotia's beech he stood,
The wond'ring throng around him croud,
    To bend th' obedient knee :
Then thinking on their Country chained,
They wept such worth so long detained,
    By Heaven's severe decree.

8.

When e'er he moves, in Sweet amaze,
All ranks with transports on him gaze,
    E'en grief forgets to pine !
The wisest Sage, the chastest fair,
Applaud his Sense, & praise his Air,
    Thus made with grace divine.

9.

How great in all the Soldier's Art,
With judgement calm, with fire of Heart,
  He bids the battle glow!
Yet greater on the conquered plain,
He felt each wounded captive's pain,
  More like a freind than foe!

10.

By good unmoved, in ills resigned,
No change of fortune changed his mind,
  Tenacious of his aim :
In vain the gales propitious blew,
Its Darts in vain Affliction threw,
  His mind was still the same.

11.

Check'd in his glory's full career,
He felt no weak desponding fear,
  Amidst distresses great :
By ev'ry want, and danger press'd,
No care perplexed his manly breast,
  But for his country's fate.

12.

For oh! the woes by Britain felt,
Had not attoned for Britain's guilt,
  So willed offended Heaven :
Thus yet awhile the usurping Hand,
With Iron rod shall rule the land,
  The rod of vengeance given.

13.

But in it's Vengeance Heaven is just,
And Soon Britania from the dust,
   Shall rear her Head again ;
Soon shall give way the Usurping Claim
And peace & plenty soon proclaim
   Again a STUART'S reign.

14.

What joys for happy Britain wait,
When JAMES shall rule the British State,
   Her sullied fame restore !
When in full tides of transport tost,
E'en memory of our Wrongs is lost,
   Nor GEORGE is thought on more !

15.

The Nations round with wond'ring eyes,
Shall see Britania awful rise,
   As oft she did of yore ;
And when she holds the Ballanced Scale,
Oppression shall no more prevail,
   But fly her happy shore.

16.

Corruption, vice on ev'ry hand,
No more shall lord it o'er the land,
   With their protectors fled,
Old English Virtues in their place,
With all their Hospitable race,
   Shall rear her decent head.

17.

In peaceful shades the Happy Swain,
With Open Heart and Honest Strain,
  Shall SING his long-wish'd Lord :
Nor find a Tale so fit to move,
His list'ning fair one's Heart to love,
  As that of JAMES restored.

18.

Tho' distant, let the prospect charm,
And ev'ry gallant Bosom warm,
  forbid each sigh to rise ;
Turn from the Ax the thoughts away,
'Tis CHARLES that bids us crown the Day,
  And end the Night in joys.

                       Cecini.

An Ode.

. . . . redeunt Saturnia regna.   Virg.

Thy deeds are such, Illustrious Youth,
Mirac'lous in the simplest truth,
  No poet's art they need ;
Let but Historians barely tell,
At Gladsmuir, what through thee befel,
  'Twill all belief exceed ;
The cause, the conduct, the success divine,
As bright, as lasting as the Sun shall Shine.

                      G

2.

For half a Century and more
Under usurping foreign power.
 Thy Father's native right
Had groned, till thou his duteous Son,
Like lightning to the rescue run,
 Chased horror's dismal night
From Clouded Britain ; Bade her Sons be free
And take that blessing under God from *Thee*.

3.

Heaven paves the way, the just approve,
An offer of such tender love
 By *Thee* to duty fired ;
That fifteen Hundred durst engage
four thousand foes ; with skill & rage
 And zealous wrong inspired :
Scarce had the raw Soldiers had the fight begun,
But all their foes are routed and undone.

4.

So thunderstruck, the Giants far'd
When impiously 'gainst Heaven they war'd
 E'er Jove regained his throne :
Such influence in thy Father's right
Hast *Thou* to Urge rebellion's flight
 And win & fix a crown.
To British Subjects peace & freedom bring,
And make them happy in their Native KING.

5.

Great PRINCE whom vict'ry can't elate,
Who doest ev'n slaughter'd foes regrete,
   Thou Glorious TYPE of Heaven
Traitors convict, to Death decreed
Are by thy generous mercy freed,
   And graciously forgiven.
Of God's resemblance you so much express
Ordained Three ruined Kingdoms to redress.

U. D.

Tho' the ungodly Senate has decreed,
That Jacob's righteous Heir shall ne'er succeed,
Tho' they resolve their treason to sustain,
And wage perpetual war e'er he shall reign :
Tho' their united force they should command,
To raze with fire & sword the faithfull Land :
Tho' they proclaim their calumnies aloud,
Varnish'd with holy Zeal t' amuse the crowd ;
O Gift of Heaven ! . . . .
Despond not to subvert their guilty Laws
The Fathers God will prop their Children's cause.
Th' almighty weighs the just, & sees them weak,
But thou implore him, for thy Saviour's Sake :
He from on high will grant thy soul's desire, ⎫
Extend thy camp & all their Hearts inspire, ⎬
With pious ardour & undaunted fire ⎭

And Thou their Leader, through thy maker Strong,
Shalt with an awful Glance abash the guilty throng ;
Those wonders will to future days remain,
To prove thou hast not paid thy vows in vain ;
But that thy sacred incense did arise
Welcom'd (as sign of love) with op'ning skies :
O may the God of order put a close,
To our confusions, and convert thy foes ;
Then shalt thou rule the Land with loving Grace,
And we thy weary train shalt rest in peace :
And now I see the Heavens extended wide,
The willing sky recoiling on each Side ;
The world's redeemer gloriously appears,
To sooth the sorrows & dispell thy fears :
High on his holy mount he sits alone,
Bright in his foot-stool, brighter in his throne ;
But oh ! his face ! whose luster is no less
Than what ten thousand Suns but faint express.
Robed with Omnipotence, behold him stand
While all his heavenly ministerial Band
At humble distance wait their Lord's command.
From his bright Eyes, flashes of rage are hurl'd
While for the Guilt of Sin he spurns the world ;
And where soe'er his angry voice is bore
It quells the mighty thunders [awful] roar :

Lo thus he spoke...... "Tho' Seas & Earth combine
" T' oppose thy right, thy title is divine,
" Thou art mine anointed, vengeance shall be mine :
" Tho' Sinful Tribes confederate with thy foes,
" Prosper awhile, yet certain are their woes :
" Let them rejoice to hear their terrors fly
" And ratling thro' the clouds invade the Sky,
" Let them confide in those and vainly boast,
" Their well caparizoned and warlike host :
" Thou art the genuine offspring of the Just,
" In me alone, Thy God, repose thy trust :
O Heavens ! Let not this vision be in vain,
But aid thy servant in this toilsome reign :
That when thro' Thee, he's settled on the Throne,
He'll hear our plaints, as thou hast heared his own.

U. D.

If you the Paths of Honour trod,
If truly faithful to your prince & God ;
If by no usual interest misled,
Nor mean revenge by disappointments bred,
But from a full conviction of the Heart
You with the righteous cause took envy'd part,
In Death's disgrace not what you were in life,
With Souls unmoved behold the mighty Knife.

Nor shudder when the kindling flames arise,
Fit incense for a Tyrant's sacrifice.
What Man can do, despise with virtuous pride,
So SOCRATES, so BALMARINO dyed,
On Kennington's dire wild the Glorious Nine
So fell, nor did at their own fate repine :
Nor with less Bravery th' intrepid Three,
Who Latest Launched into Eternity ;
Fixed to the right, and faithful to their trust,
In all things daring, save to be unjust.
   Those bright examples ever keep in view
And the bright track they pointed out, pursue ;
Remember CULLODEN ! O fatal Plain !
Crimson'd all o'er with blood of Heroes slain,
Betray'd, not vanquish'd, how they rusht on fate,
As Death the prize, and each were candidate ;
While the Proud NERO cry'd, fall on, & kill,   ⎫
Of Scotch Blood, My Boys, we'll have our fill, ⎬
He said : the Mercenary Troops obey his will. ⎭
So much the Savage Victor hath to boast,
Let him not triumph over virtue lost ;
From wild insinuations guard your Minds,
He dies a wretch indeed, whom hope of Pardon blinds ;
In time reflect, and Shun ignoble Aim,
KILMARNOCK and CROMARTIE, once the Sons of Fame,

Their honour, courage, conscience, all that's dear
Sunk in unmanly boon, and abject fear.
By their Example be each captive warn'd
The Dead scarce pityed & the living scorned ;
Barter not like the one, eternal fame,
For a few years of misery and shame :
Nor like the other to the block betray'd
Menac'd, cajol'd, the Tool of party made :
O Life ill lost ! O pardon dearly bought !
Let it not Tempt your virtue e'er in thought ;
Alone ask mercy from the powers divine,
And scorn to bend at an usurper's shrine ;
Then think for whom, and in what cause you bleed,
What endless joys will those short pains succeed ;
Wafted on Seraph's wings to those bright plains,
Where no injustice, no oppression reigns ;
Where martyr'd CHARLES in more than Royal State,
With stars encircled does your coming waite ;
Pleas'd to enstall you in the bowers of bliss,
And every worldly care and pain dismiss.

The 137th Psalm imitated by Mr Wm Hamilton, Bangours Bror·

On Gallia shore we sat and wept,
When Scotland we thought on
rob'd of her bravest Sons and all
 Her Ancient Spirit gone.

2.

Revenge, the Sons of Gallia said,
Revenge your Native Land,
Already your insulting foes
 Croud the Batavian Strand.

3.

Nor shall the Sons of Freedom e'er
For foreign conquest fight,
For power now weilds the Sword unsheath'd,
 For Liberty and right.

4.

If Thee, O Scotland, I forget,
E'er with my latest Breath,
May foul dishonour stain my name,
 And bring a coward's death.

5.

May sad remorse of fancied guilt
My future days employ,
If all thy sacred rights are not
 Above my chiefest joy.

6.

Remember England's Children, Lord,
Who on Drummossie's day

Deaf to the voice of kindred Love,
　Raze, raze it quite, did say.

7.

And Thou, proud Gallia, *Faithless freind*,
Whose ruin is not far,
Just Heaven on thy devoted Head,
　Pour all the woes of war.

8

When Thou thy slaughter'd little ones
And ravish'd Dames shall't see,
Such *Help*, such pity mayest thou find
　As Scotland had from THEE.

A Soliloquy. Wrote by Mr Wm Hamilton & found in his pocket when taken Prisoner at the Battle of Culloden.

My anxious soul is tore with doubtfull strife,
And hangs suspended betwixt Death & Life ;
Life ! Death ! dread objects of mankind's debate
Whether superior to the shocks of fate ;
To bear its fiercest ills with stedfast mind,
To Nature's order piously resigned :
Or with magnanimous and brave disdain
Return her back th' injurious gift again.
Oh ! if to die, this mortal bustle o'er,
Were but to close one's eyes & be no more ;
From pain, from Sickness, sorrows, safe withdrawn,
In night Eternal that shall know no dawn :

This dread, imperial, wonderous frame of Man,
Lost in Still nothing, whence it first began ;
Yes ! if the grave such quiet could Supply,
Devotion's self might even dare to die ;
But fearfull here, tho' curious to explore,
Thought pauses, trembling, on the hether shore ;
What scenes may rise, awake the human fear,
Being again resumed, and God more near :
If awfull thunders the new Guest appall,
Or the soft voice of Gentle Mercy call ;
This teaches Life, with all its ills to please,
Afflicting Poverty ! severe disease !
Relief from racking doubts we find in pain,
In scorn's proud insults & oppressor's chain,
To lowest infamy gives power to charm
And strikes the dagger from the Boldest Arm ;
Then Hamlet cease, thy rash resolves forgoe,
God, Nature, reason, all will have it so ;
Learn by this sacred honor well suppress't
Each fatal purpose in the traytor's breast ;
This damps revenge with salutary fear,
And stops Ambition in its wild career ;
Till virtue for it's self begin to move,
And servile fear exalts to filial Love.
Then in thy breast let calmer passions rise,
Adore thy lot, and just, absolve the Skies.

The ills of Life see freindship can divide,
See Angels warring on the just man's side :
Alone to virtue, happiness is given,
On Earth self-satisfy'd & crown'd in HEAVEN,

U. D.

Welcome to Scotia's plains, Dear injured Youth,
With thy great Sires were banished Love & truth ;
Bribes & Corruption long have filled thy Throne,
Detested arts to thy great race unknown ;
See, Britons, see indulgent Charles returns,
His virtuous soul with love for Britain burns ;
Such Love a Parent['s] heart for Sons ingrate
Keeps dormont, till repentance, e'en tho' late
Restores the unduteous ofspring to his Arms,
And all his rage with filial fears disarms;
Space for repentance Heaven affords to all,
And CHARLES like Heaven invites the prodigall :
Weep, Britons ! weep, the royal martyr's Blood
For vengeance or repentence calls aloud ;
True penitents due restitution make,
And Heaven's appeas'd, when Men their crimes forsake.
Fly then your Crimes, restore your injured Prince
And by your deeds, your penitence evince ;
Kind Heaven that pities will forgive your fall,
And late Posterity shall bless you all :

Albion once more triumph in Liberty,
From worst of Bondage, curst Corruption free ;
The Man who dares such profered grace despise
His God, his King and Country, all, denies

On Sᵗ Andrew's day. 1746.

While o'er the bowl the Gay & thoughtless croud,
In revelling celebrate the festal day
Sᵗ Andrew, Patron of Albana's Land ;
To solitary shades Macduff retired,
Thus spoke the secret anguish of his soul :
Is this a day for jollity and mirth
That wakes thy dear remembrance in our breast ?
My much-loved Country tells thy woes anew,
Opens thy wounds fresh-bleeding to our view.
How can the mind that feels for social life,
That owns the Ties of Parent, Child, or freind,
Think on thy sorrows and not feel it's own ;
For she is fallen who raised her lofty head,
[In] Majesty in the Assembly of the Nations,
She whose dear thought gave gayety to Youth,
To Glory lustre, and to pleasure transport :
Whose welfare occupied my morning's wish,
Whose welfare bade my evening mild descend :
She, she is fallen into misery, sunk in woe,
Her Laurels faded and her quiet gone.

Her Sons for every generous virtue famed,
That fire the warrior and exalt the Bard,
No more adorn her ; & no more defend.
Lo! where they measure out the fatal strand,
The hapless victims of unequal fate ;
Or rot in gaols, or on the Gibbet move,
Th' indecent scorn of their insulting foes,
While the unhappy few who escaped the Scourge
Estranged from home, and each endearment, pine.
The shunn'd dependance of a foreign court ;
A Court their free-born spirit once despised.
And in their stead, a miscreant race arise,
Who bend the prostituted knee to Baal ;
Each day with eager haste they press to kiss
The rod, warm-reeking with their country's Blood,
And Oh! dire thought, vile Parricides, they lend
Their voluntary arm to urge her doom ;
Shall I on such a day give loose to mirth,
A Day that wakes these sorrows in my breast ;
Where are her ancient venerable roofs,
Where our great fathers pass'd their virtuous hours
In manly converse and in social joys ;
Hospitable Door inviting in . . . .
The welcome Stranger to the decent board ;
A Melancholy ruin marks the place,

Hell monumental that no end was known
Of Scotland's sufferings or her foes revenge ;
Where are our Daughters, lovely as they were ?
By every charm and every virtue graced !
Their beauty's blasted by affliction's breath,
They fly for shelter to the arms of Death ;
The weeping matron wedded to despair
Indignant scorns officious comfort's aid,
For Oh ! what anguish ever equaled hers :
Torn from her Arms, she weeps her murdered Lord,
She weeps the murdered Ofspring of their Loves,
She weeps the Tender young that round her hang
Saved from the sword by famine to expire.
Behold the Gentle Maid, for whom in vain,
The modest virtues sue ; invoking Heaven
To save it's image breath'd upon her face,
To save it's image printed on her mind :
In vain . . . . . . for deaf to pity's moving voice,
Deaf to the eloquence of weeping eyes,
The fell destroyer set at nought her charms ;
And shall I then on such a day rejoice,
A day that wakes these sorrows in my breast,
No ; be the day still sacred to retreat,
To Meditation on Albina's wrongs,
To vows and great resolves of generous deeds,
When fate shall give the means of Sweet Revenge.

A Song.

From Caledonia's Loyal Lands
Where justice uncontrouled commands,
The Loyal Clans in honour's cause,
Guarded by truth, Great Honours Guide,
Came to retrieve our antient Laws
With royal Charles, Minerva's pride :
They came with freedom hand in hand,
And over the Hills and far away.

2.

To Baulk their force and stop their way
Duke Billy's sent to die or stray,
Whilst M. Wade 'midst all his Schemes
Sleeping, of conquest only dreams ;
The Bishops too, with reverend looks
Turn redcoats now, & damn their Books,
Lawn sleeves laid by, their prayers forgot,
And all their cry's a Popish Plot :
                              Over the Hills &c.

3.

Britons be firm in Britain's cause,
Assert your right, support your Laws,
Defend the truth, Great Charles obey,
And usurpation drive away.
Then Sons of War with martial flame,
You'll bravely merit lasting fame,
Great Charles will Britain's scepter sway
And Hanoverians rue the Day,
                              Over the Hills &c.

A Song made in the year 1745.

Hear my canny Highland Lad,
Relate the thing I saw, Willy,
When our brave Prince came o'er from France,
In a poor frigate sma', Willy,
Resolved his right for to assert,
To conquer or to fa', Willy :
Up and war 'em a' Willy ; Up & war 'em a'.

2.

He brought nea' armies at his back
For seven Men were a', Willy,
Then Tidings to the brave Lockiell
In haste were sent away, Willy,
He swore he'd be the first to rise,
The Last to run away, Willy,
Up and war 'em a', &c. &c.

3.

His Men cryed out we a' consent,
We'ell Banish George away, Willy ;
The next that were desired to join
Were twa Great Lards of Sky, Willy,
That they refused I dare na' say,
But surely they were Shy, Willy,
Up & war 'em a' &c. &c.

4.

Some there were to Georgy sent,
To tell him what they saw, Willy,

Appin, Keppock, and Clanronald,
Three Chiefs whose hearts were true, Willy,
Drew their braid swords & cry'd, the Prince
Shall see what we will do, Willy,
Up & war 'em a' &c.

5.

There never was sick gladness seen
As was amang us a' Willy,
The other Chiefs with Zeal as great
And hearts as loyal a', Willy,
Drew their Glymores as their assent
And cock'd their Bonnets blue, Willy,
Up and war 'em a' &c.

6.

Few there were that would na' go
Their loyalty to shew, Willy,
The Gallant Perth who long had wish'd
This happy day to see, Willy,
And for the Cause not long before,
Had been obliged to flee, Willy,
Up and war 'em a' &c.

7.

He quickly joined the Highland Chiefs
His enemies to Claw, Willy,
The *Brave Lord George was not behind   *or rather
Wi' Nairn and Gask and a', Willy,   Traitor.
They to the Standard did repair
With many Chieftains brav', Willy,
Up & War 'em a' &c.

I

We cross'd the Forth, and by my troth,
I think we were na' slaw, Willy,
The Black Dragoons who Vaunting said
That they would kill us a', Willy,
Nea' sooner hcar'd that we were near
Than faith they run away, Willy,
Up & war 'em a' &c.

9.

Our Pipers play'd from right to Left,
To force the wigs away, Willy,   *Whigs*
Then on we march'd to Edenbroe'
Where a' was ready there, Willy,
To keep us out with sword & Gun
Ick mun did fast prepare, Willy,
Up and war 'em a' &c.

10.

The cannons they stood ready charged
To play us from the wa', Willy,
The Volunteers cryed ben'a' fear[d]
For wc will slay 'em a', Willy,
What are they but a Highland Mob
Undisaplined & ra', Willy.
Up & war 'em a' &c.

11.

Their Wifcs they cryed they'll burn the Toon,
And drive from house & a', Willy,
Right Glad were they of this pretence
For fear there was, I saw, Willy,
That they had armed in their defence,
I' faith their Hearts did rue, Willy, Up & war &c.

12.

They said we'll hope that Sr John Cope,
Will come and right us a', Willy,
Then to the Cross we marched wi' Glee
The King for to proclaim, Willy,
Fou' many a joyful Heart was there
At mention o' his name, Willy,
Up & war 'em a' &c.

13.

The Wigs looked blue, and hu[n]g their lugs,
And fast did sneak away, Willy,
When Sr John Cope came from the North,
And Landed at Dunbar, Willy,
Our Army cry'd he's come at Last
We'll fight him if he dare, Willy,
Up & war 'em a', &c.

14.

To meet him then we hasted on
For fear he'd run away, Willy,
Our valiant Prince cry'd, courage Lads,
March on and follow me, Willy,
For I will never sheath this sword,
Till I have made you free, Willy,
Up & war 'em a' &c.

15.

And wha' at sick a Prince's back
Could fear or run away, Willy,
On Gladsmuir we did them engage,
Sea' soon as day did peep, Willy,
So fierce our Clans with our Glimores,
The field the[y] could not keep, Willy,
Up and war 'em a' Willy, Up & war 'em a'.

16.

We ne'er engaged our second line,
Our first did pay 'em a', Willy,
But Johny Cope and Cowardly foalk
By us were never seen, Willy,
I trow 'en a' the truth were ken'd
Their Breeks they were na' clean, Willy,
Up and war 'em a', Willy, up & war 'em a'.

17.

Lascelles had a white cockade,
By which he run away, Willy,
Our Lowland like our Highland Chiefs,
Right stoutly did behave, Willy,
And ev'ry Mun like to his Prince,
Was gallant, Bold, and brave, Willy,
Up and war 'em a', Willy, up & war 'em a'.

18.

Let Wady come when e'er he likes
We'll wrestle him away, Willy,
Our cause is just, we ha' na' fears,
Of Dutch or Danes at a', Willy,
I mucle doubt if they'll prove stout
Who lately run away, Willy,
Up and war 'em a' Willy, Up and war 'em a'.

A Song. Tune. When Britons first &c.

When royal Charles by Heaven's command
Arrived in Scotland's noble Plain ;
Arrived in Scotland's noble Plain ;
Thus spoke the Warrior, the warrior of the Land,
And Guardian Angels sung this strain ;
Go on Brave Youth, go combat & succeed,
For Thou shall't conquer, 'tis decreed.

2.

At Falkirk's famed victorious field
When Hawley proud was forced to yeild,
When Hawley proud was forced to yeild ;
Let the Applauding, th' applauding world be taught
How well Brave Charles's Heroes fought,
Go on Brave Youth &c.

3.

Tho' Thou art banish'd for a while
Yet fortune still on Thee shall smile,
Yet fortune still on Thee shall smile ;
Thou shallt return triumphant o'er thy foes,
And ruling Britain end our woes.
Then G . . . . . begone, begone with all thy race,
And to our rightful K . . g give Place.

To his R. H. C. P. of W. R . . . of the K . . . . .s of G . . . B . . . . . F . . . and I . . . . . .

En redit & Virgo, redeunt Saturnia regna.   Virg.

Hail Glorious Youth ! the wonder of the Age,
The future subject of Th' Historian's page !
Oh ! best of Princes ! best of Patriots ! deign
A Loyal muse to hail thy happy reign.
Thou, born to right three injured Nations cause,
To free the oppressèd, from oppressive Laws ;
Like Heaven thou comest with mercy in thy Eyes,
And Tears drop down when e'en a rebel dies :
Where shall the muse begin to sing thy praise,
Where fix a Period to her honest lays ;
Oh ! could my fancy with my will agree,
I still would sing, and still would sing of Thee ;
Vain are the Efforts of an artless man,
His fire extinct, and shortned half his span ;
Another Maro shall arise, whose pen
Shall place the Hero with immortal men ;
But still ye Gods ! allow me time to breath
While to my Prince's head I add a Wreath ;
While I contribute one unheeded mite,
'Tis all I can, and all for which I write.
Oh ! Godlike Man, what Angel steered thy course,
What God directed, where was thy recourse ?

Th' Usurper's fleets in Triumph cut the Waves,
The base Usurper's mercenary slaves ;
Barb'rous, fierce, & bold, they skim'd along the Main
Thyself the victim destined for their Gain ;
Yet Thou undaunted, unmolested rode,
In a small Shallop . . . . 'twas the cause of God :
But God who set at nought Th' Assyrian Pride,
Thy vessel guarded and their power defy'd ;
But say when landed on our Native shore,
What freinds thou foundst, or what could foes do more ?
Freinds, faithless some, & some by far too slow,
O'erwhelm'd thy Princely Heart with generous woe ;
While foes had destined thy devoted Head,
Like Charles the Martyr's on a block to bleed ;
Mean time Unguarded Youth, thou stoodst alone,
The cruell Tyrant urged his army on ;
But truth & Goodness were the best of arms
And fearless Prince, Thou smil'd at threatned harms ;
How happy he ! where honest views presides,
That is the Man the God of Nature guides.
Thus Glorious VASA worked in Swedish mines,
Thus Helpless saw his Enemies designs ;
Till rouz'd, his Hardy Highlanders arose,
And poured destruction on their foreign foes :

Thus soon, great S^r, thy honest cause procur'd
A Loyal race, ne'er swore, and ne'er adjured ;
A set of Men, the Terror, and the dread
Of the Detested . . . . Breed ;
A Set of men, whose worth was scarcely known,
A set of men th' . . . . did disown ;
Disown indeed, reserved for some great blow,
Some hangman's words, like loyal good Glencoe.
Those are the few, the Heavenly powers reserve,
From future slavery Scotia to preserve.
To these the ever glorious task belongs,
To vindicate their King's and Country's wrongs ;
These are the chosen band the fates decree,
To bless three realms again with Liberty.
Proceed, Great warriors ! Worthy Men ! proceed,
And latest ages shall with wonder read,
How honest, loyal Highlanders alone
Restored the injured to his long-lost crown,
Recalled great . . . . and set him on his throne.
    What praise, O Cameron, can the Muse ascribe,
To thee, from censure free as still from bribe ?
Unstained, unsullyed, in these vicious days,
The theme renewed for future Poets Lays.

The Sun shall fade, the Stars shall lose their light,
But Cameron's fame shall never suffer Night.
Bright has thyself it ever shall appear,
To all Good men, to God, to Angels dear.
Thou wast the first who lent thy friendly aid,
Of no Usurper's bloody Laws afraid ;
Thou wast the first, and thy Example drew,
The honest, loyal, honourable few.
Few, Few indeed, but mighty Hearts they had.
Then, Prince, their Leader, who could be afraid ?
So fair a Copy all must imitate,
And join to hasten the proud Tyrant's fate.
   O'er the black mountains See! the Sons of Fame
Fearless advance and catch the Glorious flame ;
They saw their Prince, they loved, & they admired
For Glory Burned, with loyalty were fired.
Ah! Virtue, little known, scarce understood,
But where the veins beat high with Scottish Blood !
Yet soon shall spread, its vigour all return,
Each Briton shall his former coolness mourn
And ev'ry Heart with equal ardour Burn,
Hail, Glourios Youth! unanimous they cry'd,
Nought e'er shall daunt us, or our Hearts divide.
Our honest father's loyal blood we share,
Thou art our Prince, thou art the righteous Heir.

K

See, See that face, where all the Stuart shines
'Tis bright divinity in fairer Lines ;
See Mild Good nature, join'd with noble Grace,
Is't not the Stuarts and Sobieski's race ?
Glorious connection ! Here the Warrior glows,
There like his great forefathers, mercy flows :
Mercy ill-timed, ill-placed ; their only crime,
To trust to[o] much, and trust it out of time.
Thou, Glorious Prince, how great was thy reply !
I come to conquer or I come to die ;
And great the conquest, if I conquer hearts,
No joy like that, the field of Death imparts.
Let proud Usurpers rule by penal laws,
Your Prince from no such right his title draws.
I come, my Britains, wrong to vindicate,
Restore her laws and save the Sinking State :
My life, while life remains, for her employ,
And die with pleasure, if for her I die.
Think not I'll punish ev'ry trait'rous deed,
My Arms are open, for my sons I bleed.
See there my father's royal word — & see
My Actions still shall with his Will agree."
    The gracious declaration issued forth
Resound glad Echoes thro' the Spacious North.

Repenting Subjects weeping own their Crimes,
Curse the Usurper, and degenerate times.
With noble ardour rush into the field,
For to such manly goodness all must yeild.
 Glengary, Keppock, Appin, Gen'rous Chiefs,
Who long have shared their widowed Country's griefs ;
Who thirty years her latest cause have mourned,
Now joy to see their antient race returned ;
Zealous they haste to meet the royal Youth,
The freind to Justice, & the freind to truth.
 Nor Good Glenbucket, loyal thro' thy life,
Wer't thou untimely in the glorious strife ;
Thy chief degenerate, thou his terrour stood,
To vindicate the loyal Gordon's Blood.
The Loyal Gordons own the generous call,
With CHARLES & thee resolved to live or fall.
 See, Athol's Duke in Exile ever true,
His faithful toils for thee, his prince, renew,
By T——t first, then by a Brother spurn'd,
Still, still with loyalty his bosom burn'd :
One of the chosen never dying train,
His Prince convey'd thro' dangers of the Main.
See how Hereditary right prevails !
And see Astræa lift the wayward Scales !

Th' Usurping Brother to th' . . . . . . flies,
While his return reechoes to the Skies.
Quick 'mong his vassals spreads the welcome fame,
Who late disdained now glory in the Name,
Flock to his Standard, and their Chief proclaim.
His Brother worthy of the Name he Bears,
(The Murray's name well known in Scottish Wars)
In Council wise, intrepid in the field,
His Prince's thunder, born with grace to wield ;
To hurl destruction on resisting foes,
And give B . . . . long desired repose.
The Murrays glowing with a generous flame,
Still of the justest praise have been the theme ;
But these I pass, their virtues speak their praise,
Nor shall be lost by inexpressive Lays.
But why, O Perth, why should I silent be,
Nor tell the world the worth that lives in thee ?
Thy hospitable doors were ever wide,
E'en to the foes by whom thou wert betrayed.
But Heaven thy guardian, stop'd the threathned ill,
And Perth preserved, and will preserve him still.
    Beloved by all see Ogilvie appears,
A man in courage, tho' a Youth in years.
Thy Acts succeeding Ages, pleased shall read,
And future Airlyes imitate each deed.

Thee Nairn and Gask, with rapture could I sing,
Still true to God, your Country, and your King :
Loyal and just, sincere as honest truth,
The same in manhood, as in early Youth.
    But while the Sun the Blew horrizon gilds,
Each minor witness to his brightness yeilds.
Strowan, Great Chief, whom both Minervas Crown,
Illustrious Bard, thou sufferer of rcnown ;
Long dimned, like rays shot from a clouded Star,
In verse Appollo, and a Mars in War.
    Menzies, received to add a nobler Grace,
To an illustrious, but forgotten race :
A race, that added to the Brucian fame,
And rises now with no less loyal flame.
    Th' immortal Grahams, but ah ! without a head,
Yet always shew that loyalty's their Creed.
Thcse, Mighty Prince, were Men, by Heaven's decree,
Reserved to catch new hope and Life from thee :
Reserved with *Thee* to pull Usurpers down,
To right thy Country, and to right thy Crown.
From Perth the Gallant Band with courage Springs,
Bent for Edina, ancient seat of Kings.
Nor dreary Wastes, nor frosts, their Ardour quell,
Nor e'en in Heart the meanest men rebel.

Welcome they come to save a ruined Town,
By Penal Laws and bigottry press'd down.
Happy Edina! now Loud Pæans sing,
Once more thou shalt embrace thy native King.
See! fortune smiles, and on thee still shall smile,
And thou art blessed while Ocean laves our Isle ;
Behold his little troop, Thy CHARLES Heads,
And (for they're brave) to certain Conquest leads.
His soldiers, he with Clemency restrains,
For Blood and robb'ry are no S . . . . . 's Stains.
Now to the East a Powerful Arm[y] lands,
And Barbarouse Cope the Scarlet Host commands ;
Furious he comes, with words Blasphemous fraught,
Blood, Death, and Torture, in each coward thought :
While C . . . . . s advances calmly o'er the plain,
In God his trust, nor is his trust in vain.
Oh! who can paint the Glories of the place ?
Where Prince, thou shou'st with more than mortal Grace,
Each heav'nly virtue Glowing in thy face.
Thy Troops, with honest Emulation Strove,
Who best should fight, and best deserve thy Love.
The Tubes which thundered horrid from afar,
But urged their Ardour to th' impending War :
Thou Giv'st the sign — impetuous they rush on,
Already in their thoughts, the Day their Own :

Nor long the Strife, for soon the Crimson sword,
Shew'd God with us : and thou next him, Our Lord.
The Dastard Foe, their safety seek by flight,
Nor longer dare to urge th' unequal fight.
Be still remembered that Auspicious Day !
In slaughtered Heaps the mangled Bodies lay ;
While Charles with generous tears their fate bemoans,
Nor checks the Sigh tho' 'tis a rebel groans.
   Oh Glorious Youth ! O Character Divine !
With what immortal Honour shalt thou shine !
" These are my Children ; Spare Ye Sons of War,
" Tho' Disobedient, yet my Children Spare."—
But Stop, my Muse ; be conscious of thy flight,
Nor dare attempt beyond a Mortal Height.
Retire with wonder and Submissive Awe,
A Virgil only can a Cæsar draw.

To Mr. J. M. on his turning Evidence.

To all That virtue's holy ties can boast,
To truth, to Honour and to manhood lost !
How hast thou wandered from the sacred road,
The Path of Honesty, the Pole to God !
Oh fallen ! Fallen ! from the high degree
Of Spotless fame & pure integrity.

Where's all that Gallantry that filled your Breast
The Proof of Sentiments you once possessed ;
Th' unbiassed principle, the Generous strain,
That warmed your blood & beat in every vein ;
All, all are fled ; once, Honest, Steady, Brave,
How great the Change to Coward, traytor, knave.
Oh Hatefull love of life ! that prompts the mind
The Godlike great & good to leave behind,
From Wisdom's laws, from honour's glorious plan,
From all on earth that dignifies the man,
With Steps unhallowed wickedly to Stray
And trust's & friendship's holy bands betray.
Cursed fear of Death, whose bugbear terrors fright,
Th' unmanly breast from suffering in the right ;
That strikes the man from the exalted State,
From Ev'ry character & Name of Great,
And throws him Down beneath the vile degree
Of Gallied Slave or Dungeon villany.
Oh Murray ! Murray ! once of truth Approved
Your Prince's Darling, by his party loved,
When all were fond your fame & worth to raise,
And expectation spoke your future praise ;

How could you sell that Prince that caused that fame,
For life! condemned to infamy & Shame.
See Gallant Arthur* whose undaunted Soul   * Lord Balmerino.
No dangers frighten, and no fears controul,
With unconcern the Ax & block Surveys
And smiles at all the dismal scene displays,
While undisturbed his thoughts so steady keep
He goes to Death as others go to Sleep.
Gay 'midst the Gibbet & Devouring fire,
What Numbers Chearfull in the Cause expire.
But what are these to thee, Examples vain,
Yet See & blush, if still that power remain.
Behold the menial hand† that Broke your bread,   † His Servant
That wip'd your Shoes, & with your crumbs was fed,   was offered his life
When life & riches, proffered to his view   & money to turn
                                                                                      Evidence, but dis-
Before his eyes the strong temptation threw,   dain'd the thought,
Rather than quit integrity of Heart   by saying, I am
                                                                                      poor 'tis true, but
Or act like you Th' unmanly traytor's part,   I will be honest ;
Disdains the purchase of a worthless life   so was executed at
                                                                                      Carlisle.
And bears his bosom to the butcher's knife.
He constant to his trust, all snares defyes
And in much Honesty is brave & Dyes,
While you tho' tutored from your early youth,
In all the principles of Steady truth

Tho' Station, Birth, & character conspire,
To kindle in your breast a manly fire ;
Freinds, reputation, conscience, you disclaim,
To Glory lost & sunk in endless Shame.
For the Dull priviledge to breath the Air
And everlasting infamy declare,
And down to late posterity record
A Name that's CURSED, DETESTED & ABHORRED.
Go Wretch ! enjoy the purchase you have gained
Scorn & reproach, may all your steps attend,
By all mankind neglected & forgot,
Retire to Solitude, retire, and rot:
But Whither Whither can the Guilty fly
From the devouring worm[s] that never die,
From inward stings that rack the villain's breast,
Haunt his lone Hours & break his tortured rest.
'Midst caves, 'Midst rocks & desarts you may find
A Safe retreat from all the human kind ;
But to what foreign region can you run
Your greatest Enemy, YOURSELF, to Shun.
Where e'er thou Goest, may Anguish & despair
And black remorse attend with Hideous stare,
Tare thy distracted soul with torments fell,
Thy Passions Devils & thy bosom Hell :

Thus may you drag these Galling chains along,
Some minutes more inglorious life prolong,
And when the fates shall cut a Coward's breath
Weary of being, yet afraid of Death.
If Crimes like these Hereafter are forgiven,
Judas & Murray may both go to Heaven.

The Paralell
Judas & Murray
Par nobile fratrum . . . .

Actions alike, alike should bare their shame
Judas & Murray both deserve the Same :
Both sold their Masters, Both alike endewed
With love of money & Ingratitude.
The Difference then between them is not great.
Hang but the *last*—the paralell's compleat.

If Heaven is pleased when sinners cease to Sin,
If Hell is pleased when Sinners enter in,
If Earth is pleased, freed from a truckling knave,
Then all are pleased when Murray's in the Grave.

A Prayer. By one of the Highland Army when at Manchester Novr 30th 1745.

Almighty Lord of Hosts by whose commands
The Guardian Angels rule their destined lands,
And watchfull at thy word to Save or slay,
Of Peace or War administer the way :
Thou who against the great Goliah's rage
Didst arm the Stripling David to engage,
When with a sling a small unarmed Youth
Slew a huge Giant in defence of truth ;
Hear us we pray thee, if our cause be true,
If sacred justice be our only view,
If right & duty, not the will of War,
Have forced our Army to proceed so far ;
Then turn the Hearts of all our foes to peace
That War & Bloodshed in the land may cease,
Or put to flight by Providential dread,
Let them Lament their Errors, not their Dead.
If some must die, protect the righteous all
And let the Guilty (few as may be) fall ;
With pitying speed the victory decree
To them whose cause is most approved by Thee.
That Sheat[h]ed on all Sides, the devouring Sword,
And Peace & justice to our Land restored,
We all together with one heart may sing
Triumphant Hymns to THEE ETERNAL KING.

A Song.

Britons, who dare to Claim
That Great & Glorious Name,
     Rouze at the Call.
See English Honour fled,
Corruption influence spread,
Slavery rise it's Head,
     And Freedom fall.

2.

Church, King, and Liberty,
Honour & property,
     All arc betrayed.
Foreigners rule the land,
Our Blood & wealth command,
Obstruct with lawless Hand
     Justice & trade.

3.

Shall an Usurper reign!
And Britons Hug the Chain,
     That we deny :
Then let us all unite
To retrieve J——s's right,
For Church, King, Laws we fight,
     Conquer or Die.

4.

Join in the just defence
Of James your Lawfull Prince,
     And Native King.

Then shall true Greatness Shine
Justice & Mercy join
Restored by the Stuarts line,
   Virtue's Great Spring.

5.

Down with Dutch Politicks,
Wigs, Knaves, & fanaticks,   *Whigs.*
   The old rump's cause,
Recall your injured Prince,
Drive Hanoverians Hence,
Such who rule here against
   All English laws.

6.

Borne on the Wings of Fame
Charles, that Heroic Name,
   All his foes dread.
He from his father's throne
Shall pull the Tyrant down,
Glorious success shall crown
   His Sacred Head.

A Song.

Thou Butcher of the Northern Clime
Thy fame descends to future time,
Your Massacres & Murders more
Than e'er were known in days of Yore.

The little Babes for mercy cryed,
Their bleeding Mothers were denyed
The lives of Husbands and their own :
Does such a brood deserve a Th——e.

2.

Must then our Prince a Wanderer be,
And all this, Britons tamely See,
Unite, Unite Ye out of Hand,
And drive those blood-hounds from the land.

3.

Bring home, bring home the royal race,
Oppression they shall quite deface ;
Then trade will flourish, Money grow,
And Milk & honey overflow.

A Song.   Made in 1746.

To all loyal Subjects glad tidings I bring
Come let us be merry and joyfully Sing,
And drink a health round to the Son of our King,
The royal and Charming Bright Laddy.

2.

Who now is arrived on our Scotish Shore,
Demanding his own & asking no more,
But to Banish the Usurping Son of W——e
Who possesses the right of our Laddy.

3.

Who Plunders our Nation of Money & Store
And to his poor Dutchy sends our English ore ;

Yet tho' we are poor, we'll never grieve more
When we have got home our Bright Laddy.

4.

Our money is thievishly Sent o'er the main,
Our trade is decaying, our brave men are slain,
Our land with high taxes is growning in pain,
And longs for the royal Bright Laddy.

5.

Oh Britons! 'tis time you Should open your Eyes,
Lest your present folly the world Should Surprise,
For favouring a Stranger, a wolf in disguise,
Who worries the freinds of our Laddy.

6.

Oppression & cruelty, Tyranny all
With Usurping G——e together shall fall,
When Britons shall give an unanimous call
To the royal & Charming bright Laddy.

7.

And then we shall have a firm lasting peace
With the Downfall of that Han——an race,
By whose means we came to a woefull disgrace
Which shall be repaired by our Laddy.

8.

The loyal Macdonalds shall then have their due,
And ev'ry Clan round them who ever stood true;
May all that's propitious befall that blest crew,
Who favoured the cause of our Laddy.

9.

May He be assisted from Heaven above,
Courageous & Loyal may all his freinds prove,
And may the best fortune attend them that love
And favour the royal bright Laddy.

10.

Let Jehovah have Glory, the King have the Crown,
O Heaven! Assist him (he wants but his own)
To Pull usurpation & Tyranny down,
And prosper the Cause of our Laddy.

———————————————————————— —

Towneley's Ghost.

When Sol in shades of Night was lost,
   And all was fast asleep ;
In Glided Towneley's murdered Ghost
   And Stood at Williams feet.

Infernal Wretch ! awake it cryed,
   And view this mangled Shade,
Who on thy perjured faith relyed
   And basely was betrayed.

Embowered in Bliss, Embathed in Ease
   Tho' now you seem to lye,
My injured form shall gall thy peace,
   And make thee wish to dye.

Fancy no more in pleasing dreams,
   Shall frisk before thy Sight,
But Horrid shouts & dismal Screams,
   Attend thee Ev'ry night.

Think on the Hellish Acts you have done,
   The thousands you have betray'd,
Nero himself would blush to owne,
   The Slaughter you have made.

Not Infants Screams, Nor Parents fears,
　could Stop thy bloody hand,
Nor could the ravish'd Virgins Tears
　Appease thy dire command.

But oh! what Pangs are Set apart,
　In Hell thou'll Shortly see
Where e'en the Damn'd themselves will Start
　To See a Fiend like thee.

With Speed Affrighted William rose,
　all trembling, Wan, & pale
Then to his cruel Sire he goes
　And tells the dreadfull Tale.

Chear up, my Dear, My Darling Son,
　The bold Usurper said,
Repent not Will of what thou'st done
　Nor be at all dismay'd.

If we on Stewarts throne can dwell
　And reign Securely here,
Thy Grand Sire Satan's King of Hell
　And He'll protect THEE there.

Verses addressed to the Pretented Duke of Cumberland
on Seeing him represented in the Print of the Battle of
Culloden in a triumphant Posture & pointing with a Seeming
Disdain at the unfortunately defeated Loyalist.

Go MONSTER, raise to Gold thy Monument,
And near the Basis place base TREACHERY
Veiled in a mantle of eternal Shame.
Then POINTING, shew the World from whence you reap'd
These Execrable Laurels which have damned
Your Name To INFAMY ETERNAL.

———————————

Other Verses addressed To the Same pretended Duke
on the Execution of the Earl of Kilmarnock who basely sued
for life by owning the Usurper's power, whereby he became a
Traytor & tho' Apprehended & Condemned for a loyalist Dyed a rebell.

The Only Rebel thou has justly slain
Was base Kilmarnock ; he alone has dyed
A Traytor to his King & Country's Cause ;
He basely sought to please thee, worst of Men,
Then Dyed Like what thou Art A SCOUNDREL.
He Died : & Dying sunk beneath a load
Of guilt immense, down to the lowest Vales
Of Erebus ; there to remain the foulest Weed
Till Death's kind hand has planted Thee besides him.

A Song.

What's the Spring, breathing Jessamine and Rose,
What's the Summer, with all its Gay train ;
What's the Plenty of Autumn to those
Who have bartered their freedom for Gain.
                    Chor :

Let the Love of your King's Sacred right,
To the Love of your Country Succeed,
Let Freindship & Honour unite
And Flourish on Both Sides the Tweed.

No Sweetness those Senses can share
Which Corruption & Bribery bind :
No calmness that Heart e'er can chear
For Honour's the Sun of the Mind.   Chor :

Let Virtue distinguish the brave
place riches in lowest degree,
Think him poorest who can be a Slave,
Him richest who dares to be free.
                              Chor.

Let us think how our Ancestors rose,
Let us think how our Ancestors fell,
'twas their rights they defended, 'twas those
They bought with their Blood wch we Sell.   Chor :

On the Departure of King James yᵉ 2ᵈ 1688.

The Great Good Man whom fortune does displace
May fall to Want, but never to Disgrace,
His Sacred Person, none will dare profane,
He may be poor, but never can be Mean.
He holds his Value with the Wise & Good,
And Prostrate, Seems as Great, as when he Stood.
  So ruin'd Temples do an Awe dispence,
  They loose their Height, but keep their reverence,
  The Pious Croud the fallen Pile deplore,
  And, what they cannot raise, they Still adore.

Verses wrote by a Lady on Seeing the Picture of the Prince.

What Briton can Survey that heavenly face
And doubt it's being of the Martyr'd race ;
Ev'ry feature does his birth Declare,
The Monarch & the Saint are shining there ;
His face would sure the boldest Wig convince, *Whig.*
He Speaks at once the Stuart & the Prince :
Oh Glorious Youth 'tis Evidently plain
By thy majestick look thou art born to reign :
My Heart bleeds as it views thy Noble Shade,
And Grieves it cannot bring thee better Aid ;

I, on no other terms a Man would be,
But to defend thy Glorious cause & Thee ;
For Both my life, I'd bravely chuse to loose,
But, now can only Serve Thee with my Muse.
Oh! were my pen a Sword, Thy foes I'd meet,
And lay the Conquered World at Charles's feet.

England's Prayer.

What! shall an Alien thus possess the throne,
Usurp another's right ; Our Church pull down ;
Outlandish Whores and Turks the Scepter Sway,
And English Valour vanish quite away ;
What! must we suffer thus ourselves to be
Cheated by Wiggs ; reduced to beggary ;   *Whigs.*
Forbid it Heaven! oh rather let the World,
Be once again into a Chaos hurled ;
Rather this Island Sink & be no more,
Than such curst mischief thrive upon our Shore :
To the Great King of Kings Let's prostrate Low
To put a Curb to Villains here below ;
To him let's humbly and devoutely pray,
To move these plagues & take this Curse away,
Set free our Country from Usurpers Strain,
And Suffer not such Wretches here to reign :

But from the British throne do them expell.
Let not such Harpies in our Kingdoms dwell,
But send our Native Prince ; grant him his right,
Whom thou hast made the Christian World's delight ;
May he To England Peace & Plenty bring,
Make him a Happy & a Glorious King :
That in his days may all divisions cease
And he triumphant reign in Wealth & Peace.

Verses occasioned by the late thanksgiving day.

Shall sham Thanksgiving never be Suppress'd ?
Shall solemn Worships prove a drolling Jest ?
Shall Albion's temples with mock'd Eccho's ring ?
And Servile Britons Io Pæans Sing ?
And must we now call out a joyful day,
To thank our God for an Usurper's Sway ;
No, Britons, No, such ill-timed praise forbear,
Doomed to a German Yoke your Trophies spare,
And for your bleeding Country Shed a Tear. '
In sackcloth veiled, and Ashes mourn too late
Your exiled King and ruined Albion's Fate :
Ye Loyal Subjects, at this deserted time,
With Sighs lament your Guilty Country's crime,
Let us this day offended Heaven implore,
To Charge this mock'ry at the Tyrant's Door,
And Strike with thunder the Usurper down,
Whilst he insulting wears our Monarch's Crown.

A Poem
On the French's seizing the Prince & conducting him prisoner out of Paris.

Degenerate Nation! Where's your Antient pride,
What helpless Prince shall e'er in you confide ;
Of injured worth no more th' Asylum boast,
To truth, to honour and to Glory lost :
Your vanquish'd foes which fatal Font'noy saw,
Those vanquish'd foes now give those victors law ;
And this inglorious peace by St Severin,
To those is triumph, and to these a Stain.
Was it for this, you run the risk of War ;
Was it for this, you sent your troops so far ;
To place a Woman on the Imperial throne
A wedded Woman there to reign alone ;
To see Glad England Mistress of the main,
Waft to her ports the Indian wealth of Spain ;
And Stuart's Son by you yourselves intic'd
To B . . . . 's Panic basely sacrific'd :
And thou whom flatterers with vain titles Crown
Most Christian King : Where, where is thy renown :
All Europe's Arbiter, shall't thou be called,
Thyself a Slave to those thou hadst enthralled ;
When in the vast extent of thy domain
Thou wilt not, dares not, can'st not entertain,
A HEROE formed on adverse fortune's plan

N

Who tires not yet to prove the perfect Man :
A Heroe who in all he underwent
In hapless BRITAIN, on his ruin bent,
Deserted, wandering, priz'd, 'midst foes combined,
Could still more freedom than at PARIS find.

While Bourbon's freindship all mankind detest
And Mourn the Victim of his interest,
Thou triumph's Glorious prince, amidst thy chains,
Each opening Eye now fixt on thee remains :
A generous people of discernment true,
resolved to crown thy merit with its due,
Will soon unbiass'd, and at length unbrib'd,
revoke the Act against a race proscrib'd :
Thy woes have changed the Spirits prepossessed,
On British Hearts thy rights are all impress'd ;
More Strong and grateful than are those of Birth,
Thy title's doubled by the right of worth :
But on the Throne remember dearest *Prince*,
What *Albion's* Annals with one voice evince :
That the proud people Jealous of their rights
And of the faith their bounded Monarch plights,
Did ne'er with Epithet of *Great* enhance
A Dastard Truckler to the Court of *France.*

On the Prince's picture.

The Christian Heroe's martial look[s] here shine
Mixt with the Sweetness of the Stuart's line ;
Courage with mercy, Wit with Virtue joined,
A beauteous person with more beauteous mind :
How wise, how good, when great ; when low, how brave,
He knew to suffer, conquer & to Save :
Such Grace, such virtues, are by Heaven design'd
To save BRITTANIA and to bless MANKIND.

The Landlord A Song. 1715.

What ails my poor Strephon, why looks thou so wan
So greizly thy beard is, so meagre thy mien ;
Hath any distemper affected thy sheep,
Or hath lovely Celia disturb'd thy soft sleep ;
That thou should'st lay here in the shade & complain,
What is it, what ails thee, and greives my poor Swain.

I was close by an Elm where his pipe & Crook hung,
Woes me, quoth the Shepherd, the Theme of my song,
Great Jemmy the Lord of the Plain, he is gone,
Hogan Mogan has seized upon all as his own.
Our rents they are raised and our Taxes encrease,
And all is because we have took a new lease.

Heavens bless our old Landlord & Send him again,
E'er famin & Poverty kills the poor Swain,
E'er the Dutch & the French our Honours do reap,
And fleece the fond Nation, as I fleece my sheep ;
So dull are my notes, and this pipe I can't play
Those tunes I was won't, 'cause my Landlord's away.

Chear up honest shepheard, asswage thy dull breast,
Leave thy sheep to themselves, like a true English priest,
Guird a Sword to thy loins, lay the sheep-hook away,
Our Landlord will come, let us clear him the Way;
See the Glass how it Sparkles, it's of true English Corn,
Here's a Health honest Shepherd to our Landlord's return.

Verses occasioned by the ringing of St Peter's bells at Exeter
on the 16 April 1748.

Murder will speak, immortal Shakespear sung,
With marv'llous organ, though deprived of Tongue ;
Thy Peals, this truth, O Peter, do proclaim
Compelled to celebrate *Brittania's* shame.
Culloden's field thy ill-timed sounds renew,
And ope fresh scenes of Horror to our view ;
Remorseless fury raging o'er the plain,
Wide-wasting massacre & thousands slain,
In his mind's Eye each briton sees again.
The baleful Tyrant of IMPERIAL ROME,

Whose lifted Dagger ripp'd his mother's Womb
Outdone in Blood, to Cumberland shall yeild,—
The modern Butcher of Culloden's field :
Whose heart unmoved could smile at Widows tears,
And branch their Sprawling Orphans on his Spears :
Nor Sighs nor prayers availed to stay his hand
While Swift destruction blazed thro' all the Land.

Edgeless for ever be thy sword in fight,
Still owe thy safety to ignoble flight :
The Pangs of Guilt Like Richard mayest thou find,
Still see the Air-drawn-Dagger of the mind ;
Haunted, like him, with murder's vengeful Cry
Like him unpity'd, may'st thou fall & die.

On the Execution [s] in London & Lancashire.   1716.

The Glories of this world to Wigs are given   *Whigs.*
Whilst the poor Jacks from Tyburn go to Heaven ;
Thus differing in their States as in their Sence,
The're damn'd & saved both by impenitence.
The Jews who're justly blamed for their Offence,
Did Christ their King betray, for thirty pence ;
The English more for Villany renowned,
Bid for their King a hundred thousand pounds,
And in their Choice to be still like the Jews,
Abjured their King & Barrabas did Chuse.

England Vindicated.

Our choice should with our principles agree,
Let force stand Neuter and the Pole be free ;
Then, Charles, might see the weakness of his cause,
Our hearts more perverse to him than our Laws :
Begone mistaken Prince, nor ever more,
think to find freindship on Great Brittain's shore ;
Wee are no subjects proper for thy sway,
Thy hateful maxims we can n'eer obey,
England shall still continue to be free . . . . . .
In Every vice and Baneful Luxury ;
Whence springs thy hope the British hearts to gain,
Who courts with every vertue in thy train ;
Vertue alass ! ill sutes our present times,
Awe us by fear or else alure by Crimes ;
'Tis not thy popery, a meer empty name,
But 'tis thy vertue that we all disdain.
Is there a minister or Man in power
Virtue could daign to hold his post an hour :
Hopes thou, from such, or were such ever known
to save a Nation's ruin by their own ;
They must oppose because it must ensue
They must find theirs if e'er thou gets thy due :
Court us in character ; religion none,
In morals like the Subjects of the throne ;

Let every vice be pregnant on thy crest,
Spare not the Infant sucking at the Breast,
Boast thy cool murders & outragious lust,
Always be sure t' associate with the worst ;
In short ; reverse thyself, & then thou'lt see
England no more shall dread thy popery ;
But be attentive to the first allarms,
And croud to Hail thee with their open Arms.

On the 29th May 1746.   By a Youth of 17 years.

Shall each vile Scribler publish William's fame
In verse as vile as the ignoble theme,
And no one Bard on Princely Charles attend,
The muses Darling and the muses freind ;   .
Where, Where, Ye Nine, are all your vot'ries fled,
Is your whole train with Pope & Dryden dead ;
That no true Britton tunes his grateful Lays,
Or strikes the Lyre to his deliverer's praise :
Ye all beheld the warlike YOUTH advance
By freinds unaided & betrayed by France ;
Yet thro' the Land his freindly banners wave,
Loth to destroy and only bent to Save ;
He profers Liberty & peace in vain,
Deluded England hugs its galling chain ;

Behold the HEROE, next on Falkirk's field,
Where brutal force to Martial conduct yeild ;
Enamour'd Victory hovering o'er his head,
While tender mercy her white flag displayed ;
Obedient Soldiers Stop't their vengefull hands,
Proud to obey their General's mild commands.
May gracious Heaven still espouse his cause,
That England may enjoy her Ancient Laws ;
Then shall we see him in the grave debate,
Treat of the important business of the State ;
Amidst the Elders silvered oer with Age
By depth of Sense & long Experience Sage :
Methinks I hear him speak while all around,
Th' attentive throng devour the charming Sound :
Hail mighty PRINCE, Auspicious Warrior hail,
Oh ! may thy virtues oer our Crimes prevail !
Thy wish'd-for presence dry our weeping Eyes,
And fix a Period to our miseries :
Then may thy royal Sire ascend the Throne,
And know no Earthly powers above his own ;
Britons shall then begin the joyful Song,
And echoing pæans dwel on ev'ry tongue ;
Should but at last that blissfull minute come,
Peace shall look down from Heaven & Plenty bloom ;

Lean discontent shall fly this happy shore,
And Usurpation vex this Isle no more;
In future times each honest rural Dame,
Shall teach her Babes to lisp out Charles's Name,
Who freed his Country from impending fate,
And by his Virtues prop'd a falling State.

On the 10th June.　By Mr. David Morgan.

Let Every Honest British Soul
With Chearful Loyalty be gay ;
Let James's Health now crown the Bowl
And Celebrate this Glorious day.
　　　Let no one care a fig
　　　For the Damned rebellious Whig,
That insect of Usurpation ;
　　　Fill a bumper every one
　　　To the glorious tenth of June,
And a Speedy restoration.

What tho' these German Renagades
　With foreign Yoke oppress us,
Tho' GEORGE our property invades,
　Our Monarch's sole possession.
　　　Remember Charles's fate
　　　How he roved from State to State,
Kept out by a Fanatick Nation,
　　　Yet came the Happy day
　　　The twenty ninth of May,
Renowned for his restoration.

Britons be Loyal once Again,
  Your president's before you,
This day that's graced with a Stuart's reign,
  Shall shine in future Story ;
      Be resolute & Brave,
      Your Country you may save,
If once you dare but be loyal ;
      Let every honest Soul,
      Either conquer then or fall,
To Establish the Line royal.

Let then your Monarch's cause prevail,
  Relieve your constitution,
Expel this race, the curst intail,
  Of William's revolution.
      Be bought & Sold no more
      By a lawless German power,
But make England a flourishing Nation;
      Let King JAMES then be your Toast
      May he Soon Adorn our Coast,
And be blest with a restoration.

Ode on the Victory at Gladsmuir 21 Sept.ʳ 1745.

As over Gladsmuir's Blood-Stained field,
  Scotia's Imperial Goddess flew,
Her lifted Spear and radient Shield,
  Conspicuous blazing to the view,
Her visage Lately clouded with despair
Now reassumed her first Majestic Air.

Such seen, as oft in battle Warm,
  She Glowed Thro' many a martial Age,
Or mild to breath the Civil Charm,
  With pious plans & Council Sage ;
For o'er the mingled Glories of her face
A manly greatness heightned female Grace.

Loud as the Trumpet rolls its Sound,
  Her voice the power celestial raised,
While her Victorious Sons Around,
  With Silent wonder Gazed:
The Sacred Muses heard th' immortal Lay,
And thus the Notes of fame convey:

'Tis done, My Sons, 'tis nobly done,
  Victorious over tyrant power;
How quick the race of Fame was run,
  The work of Ages in one hour:
Slow Crept th' oppressive weight of Slavish reigns,
One glorious moment rose & burst your Chains.

But Late forlorn, dejected, pale,
  A prey to each insulting foe,
I sought the Grove and gloomy vale,
  To vent in solitude my Woe:
Now to my hand the Ballance fair restor'd,
I wield again on high th' imperial Sword.

What Arm has this deliv'rance wrought,
  Tis He . . . . . . the Gallant youth appears,
O warm in field & cool in thought,
  Beyond the slow advance of years ;
Haste, let me rescued now from future harms
Strain fast the Filial virtue in my Arms.

I early nursed this royal youth,
  Ah! ill detained on foreign Shores,
I filled his breast with sacred truth,
  With fortitude and Wisdom's Stores:
For when a noble Action is decreed,
Heaven forms the HEROE for the destined deed.

Nor could the soft seducing Charms,
  Of mild Hesperia's pleasing Soil,
E'er quench the noble thirst of Arms,
  Of honest fame & virtuous Toil;
Fired with the warmth a Country love imparts,
He fled their weakness, but admired their Arts.

With him I plowed the Stormy main,
  My breath inspired th' auspicious gale,
Reserved for Gladsmuir's glorious plain,
  Thro' dangers winged his daring Sail;
When firmed by inborn worth he durst oppose,
A Single valour to a Thousand foes.

He came, he Spoke . . . . . . & all around,
  As quick as Heaven's swift-darted flame,
Shepherds turned warriors at the Sound,
  And Every bosom beat for fame;
The[y] catch't heroic ardour from his Eyes,
And at his side the willing Heroes rise.

Rouse, England, rouse, fame's noblest Son,
  In all thy ancient splendor Shine;
If I the glorious work begun,
  O let the crowning Palm be thine;
I bring thy PRINCE (for such is Heaven's decree)
Who overcomes but to forgive & free.

Then Civil Wars and hate shall cease,
   While plenty crowns each smiling plain,
And Industry, fair Child of peace,
   Shall in each crowded City reign ;
Then ever shall these happy Nations prove,
The Sweets of LIBERTY and LOVE.

Cato's Ghost. 1715.

From happy climes where Virtue never dies,
The much mistaken Cato's forced to rise,
Drawn on the Stage to patronise a Cause,
Which living Cato could not but oppose ;
With artful smiles the Charming pages shine,
And Treason glows in each brocaded line :
Oh! Addison, couldst thou not be content,
To sacrifice good Sense & Argument,
Hadst thou no other way to rise to fame .
And Fortune, but by wounding Cato's Name :
Mean & Injurious had but Cato lived
In Brittain's happy Isle, how had he greived,
Greived for a King struggling in Storms of fate,
And gently falling with a falling State ;
So busy rebells when they would delude,
The honest unsuspecting multitude,
Grace their rebellion with a patriot's Name,
And work their Story to the finest frame ;
Britons attend, by Cato's sense approved
And shew that you have virtue to be moved ;

That Secret plan of power delivered down,
From Age to Age, from father to the Son,
Is each man's rule of Action, & had he
Been subject to a King's Authority,
Even Cato's self had bled for Monarchy.
The field which honour moves in, is not wide,
The Laws her warrant, wisdome is her guide ;
Britons believe it, tho' the day seems fair,
Tempest & Storms are gathering in the Air,
Oppression, power usurp'd, & Tyranny,
Can never know a long prosperity;
Some mighty vengeance, some chosen Curses Sure,
Some hidden thunder in the Heavenly Store,
Is near discharging on the heads of those,
Who dare aspire above their Country's Laws.
Ambitious Demons wait their fall below,
Cæsar, Cromwell, and the proud Nassau.
Britons be just, nor sell your honesty,
Nor look on Grandeur with a dazzled Eye ;
Cæsar had all the courtly winning ways,
Cæsar had Balls, & Cæsar went to plays ;
Cæsar would whore, & rant, & drink, & fight,
Cæsar had Gold, but Cæsar had no right ;
This was the Case of Rome, consider well,

If Britain's be not just the parallell ;
But will you wanton in your Misery,
And for diversions sell your Liberty ;
You See the Man in a false glaring light,
Which Empire sheds on him, but view him right ;
You'll find him black with Crimes of deepest dye,
Murder . . . . Usurpation . . . . . Tyranny.
Oh ! where's the antient British genius fled,
Are justice, Honour, virtue, bravery dead :
Shall Tyrants revel in the British Store,
While rightful Princes beg from door to door :
Shall the Sole Briton left of royal Blood,
Be forced from Court to Court to sue for food ;
While the Usurper impiously great,
Plumes with the pompous ornament of State :
Britons, for Shame behold the wonderous youth,
With how much care he forms himself to truth,
How just, how brave, how generous & wise,
How good he is without the least disguise ;
Not all the ills that hover, can obscure
the rising glory of the royal power ;
With radiant force it breaks the Clouds of Night,
And blazes more illustriously bright ;
Such is your prince, how can you then be slaves,
To Madmen, fools, Whores, foreigners & Knaves :
Rise, Britons, Rise, your King demands your aid,
GOD & S⁺ GEORGE, can Britons be afraid ;

. . . .

restore your King and make your Country bless'd.
The attempt is worthy of the Noblest hand,
Th' attempt may every British heart command ;
Improve the lucky hours, Assert your Laws,
Nor fear to dye in such a Glorious cause ;
Cato's Experience in the world of bliss,
Assures you everlasting happyness ;
There the brave Youth, with love of virtue fired,
Who greatly in his country's cause expired,
Shall know he conquered; the firm patriot here,
Who made the welfare of mankind his care ;
Tho' Still by faction, vice, and fortune crost,
Shall find the generous labour was not lost.

Epitaph on Queen Caroline Consort to George 2ᵈ
who dyed Novʳ 20ᵗʰ 1737.

Here lies unpityed both by Church and State,
The Subject of their flattery & hate ;
flattered by those on whom her favours flow'd,
Hated for favours impiously bestowed ;
She ever aimed the Church men to betray,
In hopes to share the arbitrary Sway ;
In Tindalls and in Hoadley's paths she trod,
A Hypocrite in all, but disbelief in God :
promoted Luxury, encouraged Vice,
Herself a Slave to Sordid Avarice :

True Freindship's tender love ne'er touch'd her Heart,
Falshood appeared in vain disguised by Art;
Fawning and haughty; when familiar, rude;
And never gracious seemed but to delude:
Inquisitive in trifling mean Affairs,
Heedless of publick good, and Orphans Tears:
To her own ofspring mercy she deny'd,
And unforgiving, unforgiven Died.

The Allusion.

When Israel first provoked the Living God,
He scourged their Land with famine, plague, & Sword;
Still they rebelled; God in his wrath did fling,
No thunderbolt among them but a King:
A King like George was Heaven's severest rod,
The utmost vengeance of an Angry God.
God in his wrath sent Saul to punish Jewry
And George to England in a greater fury:
For George in Sin as much exceedeth Saul
As Bishop Burnet did exceed St. Paul.

On the tenth of June O. S.

Shall Britons still at feeble wishes stay,
And Hail with nothing else, this happy day,
Now more than half a Cent'ry rendered vain,
By vile Submission to a foreign reign;

P

Are we oppressed at home, despised abroad,
And into interests unconcerning Awed;
Where (for blood spilt & Treasures Spent) wee gain
Disgrace & Loss, and dare not yet complain;
Reflect what joy this day did once afford,
To Loyal Subjects & their rightful Lord;
When he was born, who's birth we've now in view;
who only can the joys then felt renew;
Give him his rights, & in return receive,
Such happiness as he alone can give;
For Slav'ry, freedom, & for Sufferings ease,
Trade, wealth & fame to make those blessings please.

On the Tenth of June.   By Mr. David Morgan.
A Song: tune of Old Derby &c.

Let the Loyal their Trumpets be sounding,
    Let peals usher in the Bright morn,
Let musick in Echoes rebounding
    Hail the day our Great monarch was born,
See faction aghast beyond measure,
    Rebellion with frenzy possessed,
Repine at the loyalist's pleasure,
    And obstinate grown, won't be blessed.

Old England recover your Senses,
    Your Natural Allegiance resume,

No longer exclude your own Princes,
   Quite bugbeared with horror of Rome ;
Ne'er magnify ills by suspicions,
   While you much Severer endure ;
Their patients, thus wretched Physicians
   Torment, whom right Med'cines would cure.

The Gaul on our Trade now encroaches,
   Our merchants are plundered by Spain,
All the world hence must surely reproach us,
   Who once were the Lords of the Main.
You all are grown a kick'd & cuff'd Nation,
   To such low contempt are you brought,
These the Blessings of long Usurpation,
   By Millions & millions we're bought.

Retreive ! oh retreive ! your old glory,
   Let Honour exert in your breast,
Drive, Drive all usurpers before you,
   Too long they the Throne have possessed ;
Submit to the dictates of reason,
   And render to James what's his own,
Let the thought that excludes him be treason,
   His Worth to all Europe is known.

His Scheme was the politick measure,
   That Austria and Bourbon unite,

Their Arbiter was England's Cæsar,
  Who settled each Sovereign's right.
The Ballance thus held by a Briton,
  Can we possibly longer debate,
Soon may he his father's throne sit on,
  Since we want such a head to our State.

What a Contrast is the German Bully,
  What a wild silly passionate fool,
To his primier an absolute Cully,
  His primier to Fleury a Tool.
Oh! Britain, no more be a Trimmer,
  To duty & justice resign,
Fill, fill ev'ry man then his brimmer,
  Success to the Stuarts Right Line.

A Litany for the Year 1750.

From all the Mischiefs I shall mention here,
Preserve us, Heaven . . in this Approaching year :
From Civil wars, and those uncivil things,
That hate the race of Legal Queens & Kings ;
From those who for self ends would all betray,
From saints that Curse & flatter when they pray :
From those that hold it merit to rebell,
In Treason, Murder, and in theft Excell ;

From those new teachers who've destroyed the old,
And those that turn the Gospel into Gold ;
From a high Court & that rebellious Crew,
That did their hands in regal blood embrew ;
defend us Heaven & to these realms restore,
King James the third & we will ask no more.

An Acrostick
On the right Honb^le James Earl of Derwentwater.

Dearest of men, in best of causes lost,
Envy may now her cruel actions boast ;
Rejoice then happy Martyr since life's gone,
Wear thou for ever an immortal Crown ;
Elisian Shades shall thy retreat Secure,
No more disturb'd by Lawless men in power ;
Tyrant shall vanish from our happy Isle,
When James returns, propitious heaven shall smile ;
Amidst the Croud thy Spouse & Children dear,
Their rights & Libertys from James shall share ;
Ever protected by a lawful King,
Rear up their Heads & Halleluias Sing.

Great Britain's Remembrancer :
Or
A just Account of the many singular Obligations,
So generously, from time to time, conferred upon her,
by sundry disinterested Good people, both at Home
and abroad.
A Monitory, Familiar, New Song,
in favour, chiefly, of our Foreign Freinds.
(To the Tune of the Abbot of Canterbury.)

Come ! — listen awhile, ev'ry Staunch, Honest Tory !
And I'll tell you a strange, tragi-comical Story ;
(it shall be, Sirs, however, no stranger than true)
Of the Rump,—and the Dutchman,—the German,—the Jew.
           Derry down, Down, Hey Derry down.

What a mighty support they have been to this Nation,
How worthily walked of their weighty Vocation,
My Muse shall rehearse. — If I can but prevail,
And my Countrymen dear will attend to my tale.
                          Derry, &c.

When Britain was blest with a curs'd Lord Protector,
And Satan's pure saints too whined many a D—mn'd lecture,
the righteous bore rule ;—happy, thrice Happy Case !—
for Dominion (they'll tell ye) is founded on Grace.

The Church then, what choice Nursing Fathers did nourish!
the State too—how finely, forsooth, did it flourish !
When, with unhallowed hands, both the mitre & Crown,
infernal Fanaticks made bold to pull down.

How did Anarchy then, & the wildest confusion,
demonstrate an Hellish Usurper's intrusion !
how did all honest Subjects, & faithful good folk,
then Greviously groan, Sirs, beneath the sad Yoke !

The Dutch Hogan-Mogans have oft, in great measure,
Augmented alike both our Trade, and our Treasure ;
And with Wigs and Dissenters, oft lain in the lurch, [*Whigs.*
To demolish our precious Episcopal Church.

Queen Bess, (we all know) whom they fawnly Courted,
The Poor, distress'd States, often stoutly supported,
But Lords, High & mighty, forsooth, when become,
Wrong'd Brittain might kiss then their rascally B—m !

Her Subjects they murder,—her factories seize on !
'Gainst her Kings the said Caitiffs promote horrid Treason !
Her Princes, when banish'd, they rudely reject !
But the rankest of rebells these R—gues can protect !

For which Crimes, sirs, Jack Catch might with justice have Hang'd 'em :
But, the brave Duke of York, Sirs, at Sea often bang'd 'em :
Hans butterBox tho' (we'll allow) took a strange——
A prodigious, unparallel'd kind of revenge.

Long, on this side the water the Wigs had been working ;   [*Whigs.*
And beyond Sea their Serpentine Brethren lay lurking :
Two birds with one stone the Dutch Calvinists kill'd ;
And our Isle, ever since, with Confusion have filled.

They rarely got rid of their Sturdy Stadt Holder
And, as men without conscience (we know) cursed bold are,
required, for their pious, religious, good prince,
Many Myriads, yea Millions, (mirandum !) of pince.

'Tis true, they ne'er paid for th' assistance we gave 'em,
When Elizabeth deigned from their Sov'reign to save 'em :
For Dutchmen have deemed it (we find) heretofore,
Better far to receive, than to give or restore.

And, e'er since the said Glorious, religious invasion,

These Godly, good Lubbers have still took occasion,
Ev'n, whilst in the field they've rely'd on our Aid,
To kidnap our Herrings, and Cramp all our Trade.

What horrible Hardships, what plagues without Number,
What Wars, Debts, and Taxes the Nation incumber!
In short—we've been sacrific'd, Sirs, ever Since,
But Nassau, no doubt, was a —— Politick Prince.

Yet Britain of blessings is not grown so bare of,
But Germany now too comes in for a share of,
The Bounties & favours that (all the world knows)
Or Plutus, or P——, in plenty bestows.

Poor Brittain's half broke, Sirs,—and yet, at a Venture,
To German Electors large Subsidies sent are,
'Gainst Rome we exclaim ('tis an odd kind of thing ;)
Yet gladly would make of the Romans a King.

We too boast of religion and liberty apt are ;
Yet bribe and corrupt,—to the end of a Chapter :
In other Folks' Quarrels we foolishly fight;
And foreign Connections may finish us quite.

Thus some State Physicians have giv'n us all over !—
But our wise-headed Wigsters can all things recover :
Now the Cash of good Christians they've squander'd away
Lo ! to Stock-jobbing-Jews, they have something to say.

For Mountains of Māmon the Jews are much noted ;
And perhaps may, e'er long, be good protestants Voted :
Loyal subjects, at least, so much Cash to command,
Sure, won't scruple to sell their Religion and Land.

O ! the Money ! the Money !—pray, who but a fool, Sirs,
Would not anything do, for the sake of dear Gold, Sirs,
This,—and of the Great Sampson, their wonderful love,
Our S—tsmen's descent, sure, from Solomon Prove ;

But alas ! Sirs, at length, that Great Prince turn'd Apostate,
And to Idols of Silver and Gold he fell prostrate ;
The Devil, the World, the flesh, Boys, (O sad !)
Drove that wisest of Kings (wou'd ha' thought it?) stark mad.

The Penitent Monarch (we find tho') recanted ;
But repentance, in Britain (I doubt) is much wanted,
So, your Servant, sweet friends !—I shall now say no more,
Than—God save the King !—and our Senses restore.

Derry &c.   I——— X†.

[The Time Server.]

God help the Man, condemned by cruel fate
To court the Seeming, or the real Great.
Much Sorrow shall he feel, and Suffer more
Than any slave who labours at the Oar.
By slavish methods must he learn to please,
By smooth-tongu'd flatt'ry, that curs'd court disease,
Supple to ev'ry wayward mood strike Sail,
And Shift with shifting humour's peevish Gale.
To Nature dead he must adopt vile art,
And wear a smile with anguish in his heart.
A Sense of honour would destroy his schemes,
And conscience ne'er must speak unless in dreams.
When he hath tamely borne, for many years,
Cold looks, forbidding frowns, contemptuous sneers,
When he at last expects, Good easy Man,
To reap the profits of his labour'd plan ;
Some cringing Lacquey, or rapacious Whore,
To favours of the Great the Surest door,
Some Catamite, or Pimp, in credit grown,
Who tempts another's Wife, or sells his own ;
Steps cross his hopes, the promis'd boon denies,
And for some Minion's Minion claims the Prize.

Foe to restraint, unpractis'd in deceit,
Too resolute, from Nature's active heat,
To brook affronts, and tamely pass them by ;
Too proud to flatter, too sincere to lye,
Too plain to please, too honest to be great ;
Give me, Kind Heaven, an humbler, happier state :
Far from the place where men with pride deceive,
Where rascals promise, & where fools believe :
Far from the walk of folly, vice & strife,
Calm, independent, let me steal thro' life ;
Nor one vain sigh my steady thoughts beguile,
To fear his Lordship's frown, or court his smile.
Unfit for Greatness, I her snares defy,
And look on riches with untainted Eye.
To others let the Glitt'ring bawbles fall,
Content shall place us far above them all.

[The Independent Poet.]

What is't to us if Taxes rise or fall,
Thanks to our fortune we pay none at all.

Let muckworms, who in dirty acres deal,
Lament those hardships which we cannot feel.
His Grace, Who smarts, may bellow if he please,
But must I bellow too, who Sit at ease?
By custom safe the poet's numbers flow,
Free as the light & air some years ago.
No Stateman e'er will find it worth his pains,
To tax our labours, or excise our Brains.
Burthens like these vile earthly buildings bear,
No tribute's laid on Castles in the Air.

[The Patriot.]

Stedfast & true, to Virtue's Sacred laws,
Unmoved by vulgar censure or applause,
Let the World talk, My Freind, that World we know
Which calls us guilty, cannot make us so.
Unawed by Numbers, follow Nature's plan,
Assert the rights, or quit the Name of Man.
Consider well, weigh Strictly right & Wrong;
Resolve not quick, but once resolved be strong.
In spite of Dullness, & in spite of wit,
If to thyself thou can'st thyself acquit,
Rather Stand up assur'd with conscious pride
Alone, than Err with Millions on thy side.

[On the Battle at Preston Pans.]
U. D.

Hail happy Scotland, bless the longed-for day,
That shines propitious with a Chearfull ray ;
See from her Bed thine antient Honour springs,
And lifts her crest & claps her joyfull wings :
No more shall ease her splendid form obscure,
The Scornèd victim of a foreign power.
Thy warlike Sons, a brave & generous band,
Contend for freedom to their Native land ;
And what bold hand to check thy cause shall dare
When Godlike CHARLES commands the glorious war.
In vain rebellion shakes her pointless dart,
To daunt the valour of his dauntless Heart :
Firm like a rock, He'll stem the raging tide,
Till in full triumph he victorious ride ;
But now small space the different Hosts divide
The scheme is laid on Brave Macdonald's side ;
Night draws her curtain e're the battle joins,
The rebell Army fire their outmost lines :
Not so the Clans, but in soft slumber laid
They wait the morning in their tartan Plaid.
First starts the PRINCE ere Phœbus sheds one ray,
And blest the Dawning of th' important day :
Oh Heavens, he said, While Heaven attentive heared,
This day May Justice have its due reward ;
If what I ask, if what I seek be mine,
On me may your indulgent favour shine ;

But if I aim to gain another's right
May all my forces here be put to flight ;
Amen, He cries : the Army hear around,
And Springs like lightning from the humid ground ;
Abash'd they view'd their prince & smote their breast
That he should rise ere they could leave their rest.
But soon composed they lend an anxious ear,
And listening lean his gracious words to hear.
My Freinds, he says, and drew his flaming sword,
I trust my person to your sacred word ;
This day I hope thro' God Almighty's aid,
Ye shall a free & happy race be made,
Like you unmail'd you view me here all o'er
The first in danger as the first in power.
Pursue my steps, I'll lead the warlike van,
And should Heaven frown I'll fall, the destined Man.
But may that Heaven be all their just defence,
Who fight in favour of their injured Prince.
But if success should crown our dawning hope,
And we gain conquest o'er rebellious Cope,
This is my will, this is my high behest,
In hopes for once you'll grant your Prince' request.
Let no rash hand raise his destructive blade,
To wreak his vengeance on a guiltless head.
No spite nor vengeance brought them to the field,
They fight from custom and will quickly yield :
Soon will these men be brought to own the right,
And for their lawful Prince exert their Might ;
Lead Triumph then with soft & easy reins,
The Blood's sufficient that the Vict'ry gains,
What more is shed comes trickling from my veins

Come let's advance, retrieve your Antient fame,
And Hosts shall trembling hear of Gladsmuir's Name :
For me, resolved, I rush into the field
To Die or triumph, but I ne'er shall yield ;
You see my sword, I throw the Scabbard by
A useless burden till I reign or die :
Nor shall at ease my Lazy Musket loll,
First from the mouth the flaming death shall roll :
No work is servile & no office mean,
[My] Father's & your rights [bold to] maintain :
He spoke.   The Clans a peal of joy Express,
Their Native valour kindled in their breast ;
Now joy, now rage inspire their soul by turns,
And with fresh vigour all the Army burns ;
Led by their Darling, by their soul's delight,
They came, they saw and conquered at the sight.

U. D.
[To Prince Charles.]

Be not dismayed THOU wonder of the Age,
O CHARLES ! at rebels or at party rage ;
Where e're thy royal Standard is displayed,
Thy Freinds exult, thy Foes retire dismayed.
So when the Sons of Earth for Empire strove,
And proudly waged presumptuous war with Jove,
His flaming bolts, the God in anger threw,
And to the center dashed the rebel crew.

Thy person & thy words infuse delight,
They who oppose, inward confess thy right ;
Divine that right, our fundamental laws
Assert thy claim & justify thy cause.
Shall laws of yesterday then, set aside
What immemorial time hath sanctified.
Hereditary right the Wigs disown,   *Whigs.*
Yet Brunswick by that right enjoys the Crown ;
They make their court by boasting to his face,
The Idol they have made, they can deface :
Their haughty dictates meanly he obeys,
Yields to all terms so he the scepter sways ;
Such inconsistencies will men maintain
When truth is banished & their God is gain.
Be it a King did Err ! shall that deface
The just demands of his illustrious race :
The royal English Blood with Scottish join,
Boasts not the world of such an antient line !
And tho' a strict succession sometimes failed
Hereditary right at length prevailed.
On this, Ye revolutioners, reflect,
Tremble, Ye regicides, & this Expect.
The Normans by the sword their cause maintained,
Joined to the Saxon race they justly reigned.

Edward the Second was deposed we own,
But on his glorious Son devolved the crown.
Richard the Second by like knaves misled,
His freinds dispersed, his flatterers all fled ;
Oppressed, forsaken, with ignoble mind,
Without one daring blow the Crown resigned ;
Hence Seventy years Domestick fury reigned,
Fourscore with royal Blood the land distained :
Henry the fourth Endowed with fortitude,
Wise in his counsels, all his foes subdued ;
But with his deeds his conscience was at Strife,
He mourned his Errors in decline of life ;
And mark it well : Ye, that in Change delight,
The legal Heir did not exert his right.
The Fifth stands foremost in the lists of fame,
Proud Gallia trembled at the Heroe's name ;
But o'er the Sixth, O Muse, expand a veil,
The Acts of his inglorious reign conceal :
True, he led not a lewd, adultrous life,
Nor from the Husband forced the Strumpet Wife ;
Harmless & meek, he spent his time in prayer,
(Devotion Strange) yet wronged the rightfull Heir ;
First crowned, deposed, and then a King again,
His murder then, closed his unprosperous reign.
And now again the Elder line prevailed,
And now again by Usurpation failed.

Henry the Seventh, for his prudence famed,
Th' Usurper Richard slain, the Scepter claimed ;
Wisely he joined the red rose to the white,
Then governèd by that undoubted right.
Hence sprung the STUARTS ; impious is that hand,
Which shall inalienable right withstand.
When first the Gospel was to mankind preached
For Different faith No monarch was impeached.
True Doctrine this : but forced to hide its head,
Since infidelity the land o'erspread ;
For be he Papist, Heathen, Turk or Jew,
Allegiance by the Laws divine is due ;
Authority supreme, If justly held,
By force coercious must not be repelled.
Commands illegal we should not obey,
But not with arms resist imperial Sway ;
The King by power subordinate must act,
Not He but they must answer for the fact.
Who by the king's command my rights oppress,
The laws will punish & my wrongs redress.
Thus not the one, the others can invade,
A barrier to each the Law has made.
If thousands may resist Supream command,
Should he have force, why may not one withstand ;

Allow that Doctrine, Anarchy succeeds,
And by the Peasant's hand, the Monarch bleeds.
Men sin in prosperous more than adverse times,
And plenty more than want allures to Crimes :
Lies, scandal, malice, & Erroneous Zeal
Distract the Nation & again prevail.
Pampered with ease, the populace misled,
Horrid to say the KING in publick bled.
O Deed Abhorred ! and still with threatning Hand
Dire vengeance hovers o'er the guilty land ;
Then fell the Church : rebellion was avowed,
Perjury, rapine, murder were allowed ;
Th' Estates of Nobles to Mechanics given
And ignorance was made the road to heaven.
A Daring Monster the three Nations awed,
A Compound of Impiety and fraud ;
Betrayed by those from whom redress they craved,
And by false zeal for Liberty enslaved,
At Length Hereditary right prevailed.

Then faction sculked & hid her odious Head,
Peace clapt her Wings, plenty the land o'erspread ;
Our Navy was encreased, our trade improved,
Our King revered abroad, at Home beloved ;
Thus in succession breaches oft appear,
Yet still the Crown reverted to the Heir.

And should our Crimes the wrath divine provoke
To bow the Nation to a foreign Yoke ;
Or if rebellion should the Land disgrace,
Unerring justice will at last take place.
What yet Again ! Another King Expelled,
By no example from such crimes withheld ;
Has BRITAIN sinned so far ? is it decreed
That Usurpation shall once more succeed ;
Must she with this strange fate [alas !] be curst
T' oppose her Lawfull King & choose the worst ;
Will she persist in wrong, and rashly bring
E'en from the Sink of Germany a King ;
Squander her wealth, and with the Nation's spoil,
Enrich the Hungry Hannoverian Soil ;
Reflect Ye Britons ! backward turn your Eyes,
May your oppressions teach you to be wise ;
What are th' advantages you have obtained,
What by the Glorious revolution gained ;
Justly on Popery you have exclaimed,
But has not Atheism the land defamed ;
Tindal & Toland, ignominious Brace,
Were allowed stipends to the crown's disgrace.
Oceans of blood have been profusely lost,
Hundreds of Millions have your quarrells cost.

slaves

Slaves to the Dutch, and with [no] common Sense
Mean tributaries to each petty Prince.
Laws he repeals, allowed to be of use,
Others enact[s] which slavery produce ;
Electors & Elected Both conspire
To sell their country for a sordid hire.
Be it recorded to the STUARTS praise
No grievous Taxes in their Halcyon Days.
Long from the Christian Doctrine we have swerved
Nor have the laws yet unrepealed, observed ;
Our Mercenary prelates both controul,
Preferments gained, no matter for the Soul ;
They preach rebellion, peace is not their Care,
They doff the mitre & for arms prepare ;
As when from Grapes the Tabid juice is pressed,
Awhile in peaceful rest the Atoms rest ;
Then seem to quarrell & tumultuous jarr
And fiercely combat with intestine war ;
The lightest at the top in froth appear,
The Gross subside & leave the liquor clear :
So different factions long have plagued this land,
And not for justice strove, but for command ;
But when the Nation's ferment shall abate,
And men impartial weigh their Hapless state ;

Discord

Discord shall cease, calm & Sereine our days,
The truth shall flourish with transparent rays,
Justice & peace each other shall embrace,
For then shall be restored thy injured race.
From THEE O CHARLES, Brittania seeks redress,
Innumerable Ills the Land Oppress;
March boldly on, despise Associations,
Subscriptions, contributions, combinations;
At thy Approach thy sordid foes will fly,
Knowing our Hearts, on Strangers they rely;
Dutch, Hessian, Swiss, brave only in Parade,
Compose their Mottly troops & dissonant Brigade.
At Babel thus, so will ambition blind
T' insult the Skies, Men lofty Towers designed;
Heaven with contempt their vanity beheld,
Mocked at their toil & their attempt repelled;
By various languages the Crowd mislead,
They Gabbled, raged, and in Confusion fled.

December the 20ᵗʰ 1751.

Illustrious Youth! thy freinds with transport see
The Day return that blest the world with thee.
Deign to accept on this auspicious Day,
The humble muse's tributary lay!
Early enured to various turns of fate,
Nor sunk with adverse, nor wᵗʰ good elate;
Whene'er thy soul her mortal frame shall leave,
May'st thou a never fading Crown receive.
But late, O late! with endless life be blest,
Be first in this of all that's good possest,
There, for thy virtues, boundless joy partake;
But here, be happy for thy Country's sake.
Long lost to us, O may'st thou soon return,
And chear their hearts wᶜʰ now thy absence mourn!
As Sol when envious Clouds his beams oppose,
The Clouds dispelled, with keener lustre glows;
So Thou, more great from thy retreat, arise,
With brighter Glories glad our ravish'd eyes,
And give that Bliss wᶜʰ fate, till thou art here, Denies.

[Prophetic Hopes.]

From this Auspicious night shall rise an Heir
Great like his Sire, & as his Mother fair.
Wrongs to redress & Tyrants to dechaise ;
Born to a world that wants a Hercules,
Monsters & monstrous men he shall engage
And toil & struggle thro' an impious age.
Peace to his labours shall at length succeed,
And murmuring men unwilling to be freed,
Shall be compell'd to happiness thro' need.

Declaration of

Charles   Prince   of   Wales
And
Regent of the kingdoms of England, Scotland, France & Ireland & the Dominions thereunto belonging : Unto all his Majesty's Subjects, of what degree soever, Greeting,

As soon as We, conducted by the Providence of God, arrived in Scotland, and were joined by a handful of our Royal Father's Subjects, our first care was to make publick his most gracious declaration ; and in consequence of the large powers by him invested in us, in quality of Regent, we also emitted our own Manifesto explaining & en--larging the promises formerly made, according as we came to be better acquainted with the inclinations of the people of Scotland.   Now, that it has pleas'd God so far to Smile on our undertaking, as to make us master of the Antient Kingdom of

Scotland, we judged it proper, in this publick
manner, to make manifest what ought to fill the
Hearts of all his Majesty's subjects, of what
Nation or province soever, with Comfort and
Satisfaction. We therefore hereby, in his
Majesty's Name declare, that his sole intention
is to reinstate all his subjects in the full enjoyment
of their Religion, Laws, & Liberties; And that our
present attempt is not undertaken in order to
enslave a free people, but to redress & remove
the encroachments made upon them; not to
impose upon any a religion they dislike, but to
secure them all the enjoyment of those which
are respectively at present establish'd among
them, either in England, Scotland, or Ireland; &
if it shall be deemed proper, that any further security
be given to the establish'd Church or Clergy,
we hereby promise, in his name, that he shall
pass any law, that his Parliament shall

judge necessary for that purpose. In consequence
of the rectitude of our royal Father's intentions,
we must farther Declare his sentiments with
regard to the National Debt. That it has been
contracted under an unlawful Government, nobody
can disown, no more than that it is a most heavy
load upon the Nation; yet in regard that it is
for the greatest part due to those very subjects whom
he promises to protect, cherish & defend, he is
resolv'd to take the advice of his Parliament concerning it, in which he thinks he acts the part of a
just Prince, who makes the Good of his people the
sole rule of his Actions. Furthermore We here in
his Name declare, that the same rule laid down
for the Funds, shall be followed with respect to
any Law or Act of Parliament since the Revolution;
and, in so far as, in a free & legal Parliament, they
shall be approved, he will confirm them. With
respect to the pretended Union of the two Nations

the King cannot possibly ratify it, since he has had repeated remonstrances against it from each Kingdom ; & since it is incontestable, that the principal point then in view was the exclusion of the royal Family from their undoubted right to the Crown, for which purpose the grossest corruptions were openly used to bring it about. But whatever may be hereafter devis'd for the joint benefit of both Nations, the King will most readily comply with the request of his Parliaments to establish. And now that we have, in his Majesty's Name, given you the most ample security for your religion, properties & Laws, that the power of a British Sovereign can grant ; We hereby for ourselves, as Heir Apparent to the Crown, ratify, & confirm the same in our own Name, before Almighty God, upon the faith of a Christian, & the Honour of a Prince. Let me now expostulate this weighty matter with

you, my Father's Subjects, and let me not omit
this first Publick opportunity of awakening your under-
standings, & of dispelling that Cloud, which the
assiduous pens of ill designing Men have all along,
but chiefly now, been endeavouring to cast on the truth.
Do not the Pulpits & the Congregations of the Clergy,
as well as your weekly papers, ring with the Dreadfull
threats of Popery, Slavery, Tyranny, & Arbitrary power,
which are now ready to be imposed upon you, by
the formidable powers of France & Spain? Is not
my royal Father represented as a blood thirsty
Tyrant, breathing out nothing but destruction to all
those who will not immediately embrace an odious
religion? Or have I myself been better used? but
listen only to the naked truth ....

I, with my own money, hired a vessel,
ill provided with money, Arms, or freinds; I arriv'd
in Scotland attended by seven persons; I publish
the King My Father's Declaration, & proclaim his
Title, with pardon in one hand, & in the other Liberty

of Conscience, & the most solemn promises to grant
whatever a free Parliament shall propose for the
Happiness of a people. I have, I confess the greatest
regard to adore the Goodness of Almighty God, who
has, in so remarkable a manner, protected me
& my small Army thro' the many Dangers to w^ch
we were at first exposed, & who has led me in
the way to victory, and to the Capital of this
antient Kingdom amidst the Acclamations of the
King my Father's Subjects : why then is so much
pains taken to spirit up the minds of the people
against this my undertaking. The reason is obvious,
it is, lest the real sense of the Nation's present
sufferings should blot out the remembrance of
past misfortunes, & of the outcries formerly rais'd
against the royal family ; whatever miscarriages
might have given Occasion to them, they have been
more than attoned for since ; & the Nation has now
an opportunity of being secured against the

like for the future. That our Royal Family has suffered exile during these fifty seven Years, every Body knows; has the nation during that Period of time, been the more Happy or flourishing for it? Have you found reason to love & cherish your Governors, as the Fathers of Great Baittain & Ireland? Has a family, upon whom a faction unlawfully bestowed a Diadem of a rightful Prince, retained a due sense of so great a trust & favour? Have you found more Humanity & Con-descention in those who were not born to a Crown, than my royal forefathers? Have their Ears been open to the Cries of the People? Have they, or do they consider only the interest of these Kingdoms? Have you reaped any other Benefit from them, than an immense load of Debts? If I am answered in the affirmitive, why has their gouerment been so often railed at in all your publick assemblies? Why has the Nation been so long crying out in vain for redress against the Abuses of Parliaments, upon the Account of their long duration, the multitude of Place-Men, which occasions their venalty, the introduction of Penal Laws, and in general, against the miserable situation of the Kingdom at home, & abroad? All these, & many more inconveniences must now be removed, unless the People of Great Brittain be already so far Corrupted, that they will not accept of Freedom when offered them; seeing the King, on his restoration, will refuse nothing a free Parliament can ask, for the Security of their religion, Laws & Liberty of the People. The fears of the Nation from the powers of France & Spain appear still more vain & groundless; My Expedition was undertaken unsupported by either: But, indeed when I see a foreign force brought by my Enemies against me, & when I hear of Dutch, Danes,

Hessians and Swiss, the Elector of Hanover's Allies, being called over to protect his goverment against the King's subjects, is it not high time for the King, My Father, to accept also of the assistance of those who are able, & who have engaged to support him? But will the world, or any Man of sense in it, infer from thence, that he inclines to be a tributary Prince, rather than an independent Monarch? Who has the better Chance of being independent on foreign powers? He, who with the aid of his own subjects, can wrest the Government out of the hands of an intruder; or he, who cannot, without Assistance from abroad support his Gouerment, tho' establish'd by all the Civil Power, and secured by a strong military force, against the undisciplin'd part of those he has ruled over so many Years? Let him, if he pleases, try the experiment, let him send off his foreign Hirelings & put the whole upon the issue of a Battle ; I will [trust] only to ye King my father's Subjects, who were or shall be engaged in mine & their Country's Cause : But notwithstanding all the opposition he can make, I still trust in the justice of my cause, the Valour of my Troops, & the Assistance of the Almighty, to bring my enterprise to a glorious Issue.

It is now time to conclude, & I shall do it with this reflection. Civil warrs are ever attended with rancour & ill will, which party-rage never

the mind of

fails to produce in ʌ those, whom diffcrent interests, Principles or views, set in opposition to one another ; I therefore earnestly require it of my freinds, to give as little loose as possible to such Passions ; this will prove the most effectual means to prevent the same in the enemies of our Royal Cause. And this my Declaration will [shew] to all posterity the Noble-ness of my undertaking, and the Generosity of my intentions.

Given at our Palace of Holyroodhouse, the tenth of October One Thousand Seven Hundred and Forty five.

C. P. R.

By his Highness's Command

Jo. Murray. Sec.

A Letter to the Arch Bishop of York : Humbly offering to his Grace's Solution some Doubts & Scrupules suggested by his late speech to the Grand meeting of the County of York, called to subscribe an Association for supporting the German Government in England.

Amicus Aristoteles, Amicus Plato ; sed magis Amica veritas. Magna est veritas et Prevalebit.

My Lord,

I have read your Speach to the Grand meeting of the County of York, on the 24th ult. with all the attention I was capable of & with that teachable Disposition with which the faithful ought to listen to the admonitions of such spiritual Guides as do not claim implicit faith & blind obedience, as this is, I hope, the Case with you ; & as the Nature & Design of your High office makes you an instructor of the ignorant, & a helper of the joy (tho it gives you no Dominion over our Faith) of Christians, your Grace will forgive me to lay before you some of the Difficulties which occurr'd to me upon reading that paper : Difficulties that must be removed e'er I can with safety to my soul enter into the Association pro-

posed : for I am convinced, that whatever is not
done in faith (or a full persuasion of the Lawful-
ness of what we Do) is Sin ; & that Bonds &
combinations of such importance ought to be enter'd
into very advisedly and [as good men come
to the Highest sacrament, that of Christ['s] Body
& Blood] with a firm trust in God's Mercy, & with
a quiet Conscience. And therefore it is, that
I apply to your Grace, as the fittest Person,
to quiet those Doubts & Scruples you haue
awakened. I am not unacquainted with the
Character you have acquired by your lear-
ning, & other endowments ; nor with that awful
regard which is Due to your place & Dignity : I would not willingly fall short in
the respects due to either, & therefore, if this
letter is found written with less Ceremony
than you are accustomed to meet with, from

people below your own rank, I beg your Grace
will ascribe it to my zeal for truth, and for the
Honour of the Church of England, which I cannot
see affronted & abused by her own members, of what
order soever, without just Concern, & even some
mixture of indignation. From the Paper before
me, I Humbly conceive, your grace has not been
duly informed of some facts you have ventured
to affirm. You have shewed a Disposition
to renounce & give up some of the distinguishing
Doctrines of the Church over which you preside
& which you have sworn to maintain ; & indeed
throughout the whole of your pathetic exhor-
tation, there appears more of the Soldier, than
of the Bishop ; more of the Spirit of Elias, than
of Jesus Christ. I was sorry to find your
Grace's Temper so soon ruffled, & your Zeal

getting so much the ascendant of your charity.
The wrath of Man worketh not the righteousness
of God ; and yet you are not got beyond the third paragraph of your Discourse, when you are very
angry with the Scots Army, whom (in your passion) you represent as a set of wild & desperate
ruffians. A hard name, intended, no doubt, to
convey into your Audience a very unfavorable
Idea of those Men, & to strike the utmost abhor-
rence. Sure, your Grace has not known, that
the best Blood of Scotland is in that Army ;
& that many of the Nobility & Gentlemen of that
Kingdom (as illustrious by their many Virtues,
as by their Birth & Quality) have judged it their
duty to attend that Standard, or you would not
have branded them with such Terms of reproach & ignominy. I must, therefore, suppose

your Grace had none in view but Highlanders, when you gave that bad Character : & even to them it will not apply : if you had represented them as men bold, Hardy, enterprising, accustomed to hardship & fatigue, fearless of Danger, under strong convictions of the justice of their Cause, & resolv'd to conquer, or Die in the attempt, you had done them justice ; but to scold them as rascals, & ruffians, was not fair Dealing, either with respect to them or your Audience. If my information is just, as I have reason to think it is, they are Men very different from what you would have us believe them. If the Glenco men could march close by the Earl of Stair's House, without hurting a Chicken, even where they had ground for all the resentment which the remembrance of a Bloody massacre could inspire ; if there

U

has scarce one of that Army been seen Drunk, or hear'd to swear an oath ; if, before the late Action, while General Cope's Troops were blaspheming, The Highlanders were devoutly sending up their prayers to God, for his Direction & assistance ; and, after the Action, they return'd their thanks to Heaven, ascribing all the glory of a Compleat victory to the great God of Battles, to whom they acknowledg'd it due ; If all this is true, as I am well assured it is, your Grace had better spared these terms of reproach. At any rate, My Lord, scolding does not seem the proper language of the Clergy : Nor should such words come from an Archie- piscopal Throne. The Universal Bishop, and Head of the Church, saluted his Betrayer with the soft Compellation of freind ; and if the Angels of the Churches would copy from the Angels in Heaven, your Grace might have learned better

Temper & greater Decency from S^t. Michael, who Durst not bring a railing accusation even against the Devil. But, to pass this, as only a failure in the Decorum becoming your exalted Station, your next Paragraph presents us with something worse ; no less than a glaring Departure from truth and common Honesty. There your Grace tells us of certain Evidence which every Day opens more & " more, that these commotions in the North, are " but part of a great plan concerted for our ruine ; " and that they have begun under the Countenance, " & will be supported by ye forces of France & Spain." The shortest & most satisfying answer to this charge will be, to give you the Testimony of one who must be allowed to know better than you the secret Springs of this undertaking, & what encouragement they have from foreign powers ; & whose authority must be acknowledged not inferior to any upon Earth.

Even your Grace will not Deny, that the word of a Prince is equal to that of a Bishop. In a declarration of the intention of his royal Highness given at his Palace of Holyrood-House the 10th instant, after he has solemnly promised, before Almighty God, upon the faith of a Christian, & the Honour of a Prince, to maintain the religion Laws & Liberties of his people; not to impose upon any a religion which they Dislike, but to secure them all in the enjoyment of those which are respectively at present establish'd amongst them, either in England, Scotland, or Ireland; even to refer the consideration of the National Debt (tho' contracted under an unlawful gouernment) to the representatives of the Nation, and, in general, to refuse nothing that a free Parliament can ask for the security of the Religion, Laws, & Liberties of his people: after all this, he adds

a paragraph, which I shall transcribe entire,
as that excellent Paper may not yet have come into
your Grace's Hands. " The Fears of the Nation
" from the Powers of France & Spain appear still
" more vain & groundless. My expedition was
" undertaken unsupported by either ; but, indeed,
" when I see a foreign force brought by my enemies
" against me, & when I hear of Dutch, Danes,
" Hessians & Swiss, the Elector of Hanover's allies,
" being called over to protect his Gouernment
" against the King's Subjects, is it not high time for
" the King my father to accept also of the
" assistance of those who are able, & who have
" engaged to support him ? But will the world,
" or any one man of sense in it, infer from thence,
" that he inclines to be a tributary Prince,
" rather than an independent Monarch ? Who

A Letter

" has the better Chance of being independent on foreign
" Powers? He who, with the Aid of his own Subjects,
" can wrest the Government out of the Hands of an
" intruder? Or He who cannot, without assistance from
" abroad, support his Gouvernment, tho' establish'd
" by all the Civil power, & secured by a Strong Military
" force, against the undisciplined part of those he
" has ruled over so many years? Let him, if he
" pleases, try the Experiment : let him send of[f]
" his foreign Hirelings, & put the whole upon the
" issue of a Battle ; I will trust only to the King
" my father's Subjects, who were, or shall be engaged
" in mine & their Country's Cause. But, Notwith-
" standing all the Opposition he can make,
" I'll trust in the justice of my Cause, the Valour
" of my troops, & the assistance of the Almighty,
" to bring my enterprize to a glorious issue."

When your Grace has compared this Declaration of
a Prince, with what you have ventured to bring
forth, & balanced the Credit Due to either side, I
dare say, you'll be ashamed of so hardy an Affir-
mation, and of so base an attempt to impose
upon the Credulity, & alarm the fears of your People,
by your own vain conceits, & groundless jalousies,
if I may call them by so soft a Name. I dare be
bold to say, I love the Religion, Laws & Liberties
of my Country, as sincerely as any man in it can
do ; but then I think these are too sacred to be
maintained by bad means. I would not speak
wickedly for God, nor talk deceitfully for Him,
Job xiii. 7. Nor can I (without some struggle) forbear
repeating the Psalmist's words : Let the lying
Lips be put to silence, which cruelly, Disdainfully
and despitefully speak against the Righteous.

This gave me a Specimen of your Grace's Veracity, & strict regard to truth ; but I did not begin to suspect your Prudence, till I came to your fifth paragraph, wherein (to my great surprise) you have the Confidence to bring forth a number of facts, which every man that Heared you knew to be false, and which had been often, & solemnly disputed & denied by some of them in Parliament, and by many more out of it. Prithee, my Lord, is Canterbury so much better than York, that your Appetite for the Single Ecclesiastical Dignity higher than what you now possess, has made
                    the virtue &
you forget ∧ the Character of a Churchman ? Was you in jest or Earnest, when you insulted the common sense & universal feeling of the Nation, by saying "we are now blessed "with the mild administration of a just

" and Protestant King, who is of so strict an
" Adherence to the Laws of our Country, that not an
" instance can be pointed out, during his whole
" reign, wherein he made the least attempt upon
" the Liberty, Property & religion of a Single
" person." My Good God deliver my soul
from lying Lips, & from a Deceitful Tongue.
My Lord, I am not accustomed to despise Dominion, or speak Evil of Dignities. Tho' I am
convinced in my conscience, the reigning
Prince has no good right to the throne he sits
on ; yet I consider him as a Gentleman, a Prince,
a relation of our true & Natural King (tho' very
distant, more than fifty removes from being the
nearest in Blood to y⁰ Crown) ; and therefore would
not have chosen to use freedoms with his Character,
nor to have brought forth unsavoury truths of
his administration, if you had not forced me to it.

But Prithee, My Lord, did the Excise-Scheme, the Number & rigour of Penal Laws, & standing Armies, the Swarms of Place-men and Pensioners, and the Venality of Parliaments, threaten no danger to the liberty of the Nation? Did the management of the charitable Corporation (whereby the partner of his bed was enriched) do no harm to the Property of any individual? Does the immoderate increase of National Debts & Taxes, lavish'd away to support useless fleets & Armies, employed in Foreign quarels wherein Britain has no Concern, or laid out in the Purchase of Bremen & Verden, and in the Aggrandizement of Hanover; have these done no hurt to the property & prosperity, to the Honour & Trade of the Nation? And as for Religion, I think I may appeal to Your Grace

who ought to know more than I do, whether it be
at present in a thriving condition, either as to the realities,
or bare profession of it? whether Deism & infidelity,
Luxury & perjury, & prophaneness of all sorts, have not
grown to an enormous height, & found not only impunity,
but encouragement from this mild Administration?
Whether the most sacred offices, & highest Dignities
in the Church have not been set to Sale; or bestowed
more with respect to Party-interest than to real
merit & fitness? Whether, to offer but one instance
out of Many, your Brother of Winchester does not
well deserve something else than the first Benefice in
England, when, by his plain account of the Sacrament,
and his measures of Submission to Sovereign Powers,
he has attempted to Burlesque the most sacred insti-
tution of Christianity, & a Distinguishing Doctrine

of the Church? & in short, I dare appeal to your
Grace, if, in your Conscience & secret thought
you are not convinced, that religion in Britain
has suffered, & visibly Declined, both as to its power
& form, by that very Revolution that was pretended
to be contrived for its purity & preservation? If
these things are so, with what face could you tell
your people, that no attempt has been made upon
their Liberties, properties, or religion? 'Tis true,
you have expressed the thing warily, & may hope
to ly snug under the shelter of Equivocation, that no
such attempts have been made upon the Liberty &c.
of any single Person. But what then? If such attempts
have been made upon the whole Nation, does not
that comprehend, & must it not affect every individual? Is he less guilty, who burns down a
forest than he who lays his Ax to the root of a

single tree? Perhaps, your Grace, may hope to
save your Credit, by accusing the Ministry, & telling
us gravely, it is the Law of England, that the King
can do no wrong. Be it so, my Lord: But was not
this the Law of England fifty Seven Years ago as
well as now? And yet you know what happen'd then?
In the remaining parts of your Speech, you go on
with great fervour, & a flow of eloquence, to persuade
your flock to unite in common Measures, Associations, contributions, &c. for our Defence against
this prodigious ruin; & you generously undertake,
that your Clergy shall distinguish themselves, by
their Ardour, Zeal & Liberality, according to their
Circumstances, on this important Occasion.

But it is very remarkable, you have never once,
in all this long Speech, recommended to your
Clergy or people, repentence & Humiliation,

fasting & Prayer, as proper means of averting threatned ruin. One would have expected some mention of these from a Bishop's Chair, especially after so much noise made about the Danger of religion. Was it not as expedient to have had recourse to the Divine Author of our Holy Religion for his protection & Support, as to have put your trust only in the Arm of flesh? But your Grace was resolved to be consistent, & of a piece. You had all along shewed more of the peer than of the Prelate, & would not now mingle Characters. Or, perhaps you industriously avoided to touch this Delicate point, from a secret conviction upon your mind, that such incense would be abominable to God, & such prayers turn into Sin, & a snare to you; & that the absolute Disposer of Empires & Kingdoms, the invincible asserter of truth & right, would not

accept of Humiliations, nor Hear the prayers
offered for the support of Usurpation & rebellion,
of oppression & Violence. But there is another
Omission in your performance, which I humbly
think your people had reason to take amiſs, viz.
that you labour to engage them in great expences,
& dangerous Associations, without any attempt to
satisfy them as to the quarrel, or the justice of
the Cause, in which they were to venture their
Lives, their fortunes, & their Souls. Had this
speech come from a Crafty Statesman, or a
Designing Tub-preacher ; from Hugh Peters,
or a Shaftsbury, from a Tindal or a Toland,
such men as had no hopes or fears beyond this
present world ; to have rung the Crime [qy—Chime?] of Male-
Administration, excellent Constitution, &

a present Happy Establishment, was all that could be expected from Gentlemen of their Modern religion. But one would have thought a Christian should have gone Deeper, & touched the Point of Conscience; as Doubtless you would, if you had not found it so warm as to burn your fingers. You had told us, indeed, in the beginning of your Speech, that "the Pretender's Son is in Scotland." Had it not been worth while to examine what his pretensions are? What if it should appear, upon summing up the Evidence, that the Laws of God & nature, & the fundamental Laws & Constitution of England, give him right to the Allegiance of those very people you have been spiriting up to oppose him? If this is the Case, (as, I dare say, the best, & wisest, and greatest part of the people of Brittain are now convinced it is) then the unatural Rebellion lies where you did not suppose it, & the Bishop must appear in a very odd light, who employs his great Talents, & all the influence of his place, to support a guilty, ruinous Usurpation, & persuade the people he ought to lead on in the ways of truth & Duty, to eternal rest & happiness, to engage themselves in a Damnable Treason & Parricide? It is presumed, Your Grace will not Dispute what is so generally believed, that nonresistance to sovereign powers has been the Constant Doctrine of the Church of England ever since her happy Reformation from Popery. For proof of this, it would be equally tedious and needless to refer your Grace to (what

you are so well acquainted with) the Sermons
& other writings of those shining lights of our
Island, Doctors Overald, Ferrer, Hooper,
Coverdale, Jewell, Hooker, Bramhall, Andrews,
Usher, Jackson, Saunderson, Hammond,
Chillingworth, Barrow, Sancroft, Stillingfleet,
all from the excellent Cranmer, down to the
late worthy & eminent Archb^p Sharp, and
others your predecessors, in the Sea of York.
But we may shorten this Argument, by appea-
ling to an Authority you have already sub-
mitted to, & therefore must not dispute.
Your Grace could not be raised to your present Dignity without subscribing to the Articles of the Church of England. In the
thirty fifth of these Articles it is affirmed,

" that the Books of Homilies do contain a
" Godly & Wholesome Doctrine, & necessary
" for these times." In one of these Homilies (that
of rebellion) the Doctrine of Nonresistance to
Souereign Powers is taught in terms as full
& Strong as could possibly be devised. There
we are told, " We must be subject for Conscience
" sake, & not only for Wrath : that our Obedience
" is due to our Princes not only to the wise, the
" Good & Gentle, But even to the froward, to
" undiscreet & Evil Gouernors : and that, on no
" pretence what soever we can resist or rebel
" against Lawful Authority, as we will answer
" to God, & under the pain of Damnation."

And it is Observable, that, in the Several
parts of that Homilie, the Church often mentions the King under the Denominations of

our Lawful & Natural Prince, as if (the one being exegettical of the other) she hereby meant to teach us, that the Crown of England is Hereditary, and the Succession to it Lineal; so that none who wears it can be our Lawful, unless (by proximinity of Blood) he is our Natural Prince too. Moses seems to have suggested this to the people of Israel, "that, as the King to be set over them " should not multiply Horses, nor Wives, Nor " Silver & Gold; so he should be, not a Stranger, " But of their Brethren, & whom the Lord should " chuse," Deut. 17. 15, 16, 17. That this is the true meaning & intendment of the Church of England, is farther Evident from the Offices of the 30th of Jan. & 29th of May, wherein also the faithful are taught to acknowledge, before God, that King Charles the 2^{d} even when in Exile, even when abjured

jured & proscribed, "was the undoubted Heir
" of the Crown, and that the throne did of right
" belong to him." I dare say, Your Grace could
never read those Offices, without some sacred
feeling of the Sufferings of the Royal Family
in a Parallell Case, & a conviction that they
have met with hard measure in being so long
kept abroad. This may suffice to be said to you,
as you are a prelate in the Church; if it were not
to be tedious to your Grace, I should now address
you as a Peer of the Realm, & beg you would so
consider the Laws of England; such Laws, I
mean, as have been made by our Kings &
Parliaments together. For I cannot admit
those Statutes that have past without legal
Authority (which is an Essential part of the
Legislature) can have the Authority of Laws;

Nor will your Grace attempt to defend the old ridiculous Circle, of the Laws making a King, &
then the King's giving a Sanction to the Laws.
I might refer Your Grace to the Corporation Act,
(13. Car. 2ᵈ Stat. 2. Sect. 5); to the Militia Act (,13 &ᶜ.
14.) Car. 2ᵈ Cap. 3.); & to the Act of Uniformity,
(*ibid.* Cap. 4.); by all which it is declared, "that
"it is not Lawful upon any pretence whatsoever,
"to take up arms against the King, &c." But,
to save time, I shall only recommend to Your
Grace's Serious considerations, that Act (12. Car.
2ᵈ Cap. 30.) which is appointed to be read in
all the Churches in England once every Year;
whereby it is Declared, that, by the undoubted &
fundamental Laws of this Kingdom, neither the
Peers of the realm, nor the Commons, nor both
together, in Parliament or out of Parliament, nor

the   people,   collectively   or   representatively,
nor any other persons whatsoever, ever had, have,
hath, or ought to have any Coercive power over
the Persons of the Kings of this Realm.   Now,
My Lord, I agree with your Grace, that the Constitution of y⁰ Gousernment is the best in the world.
But where shall one Learn, or hope to find
the true Constitution of England, if it is not in
the Doctrines & Offices of the Church & the Laws
of the Land? for to measure it by times of Anarchy or Usurpation, is like judging of a Man's
Health by feeling his pulse in a fever.   If nonresistance is the Doctrine of the Church of England,
& if this Doctrine is established on the word of
God, on the expressed precepts, & examples
in Holy Scripture (as this Church says it is),

then 'tis plain, it cannot vary with time & Circumstances, but was as much our Duty at the Revolution as it is now. If the Doctrines of the Church, & the Laws of the Kingdom do concur to assure us, that Subjects must not take Arms, or rebel against their King, on any pretence whatsoever ; that the Crown of Britain is Hereditary ; & the Succession to it Lineal : Then it is Evident, to an Ordinary understanding, that ye revolution in 1688 was against all the rules of our established Religion & Policy : And if it was faulty at first, the long Continuence of it does not mend the matter ; for it is an allowed Maxim, Quod ab initio est Vitiosum, tractu Temporis non convalescit. Upon the whole, I cannot help thinking, Your Grace is brought into a Difficulty, from which I wish you may extricate yourself in the best & safest way. For either the Throne of

England is Hereditary, or it is Elective. Chuse
you, my Lord, which of the two. If it is hereditary,
'tis certain, the Prince who sits in it at present,
has no right; & that your Speech to your People
was inept, seditious, treasonable, & Damnable,
being meant to Spirit up an opposition to the
true & rightful Heir. If it is Elective, & the free
gift of the people, then the reasons which
exist at present for a change of Masters (ari-
sing from a long Course of Male-Administration,
& that inevitable Slavery & ruin which must
otherwise ensue) are as many & as strong now
as ever they were at any time since England
was a Nation ; & ought to Determine you instantly
to receive with Chearful Hearts, & open Arms
that Glorious Prince who now claims it as his
due. Tho' he had not been born to gouvern us,

he ought to be our Choice, as being the person on earth who bids fairest to make us free & a happy people.

I beg your Grace will not make light of this adress, the Subject is of the utmost importance, & deserves to have fallen into better Hands. You & I are now advancing fast in Years, and must ere long (& how soon, none of us can tell) make our Appearance before the Great judge of the world, to give a Strict Account of what we have done in the Body. Let us not, therefore, be misled from the straight paths of justice & truth, by any worldly views or selfish considerations whatsoever, but so acquit ourselves in our several Offices & Capacities, as we may best answer at that awful tribunal.

If you honour · me with a return, you

may make it as publick as this, & it will come
into the Hands of

My Lord,

Your Grace's Most

Faithfull Son & Servant

Philalethes.

From my Closet,

Oct. 15th 1745.

Notes and Illustrations.

NOTES AND ILLUSTRATIONS.

Page 1.　*A Song.　Tune Holloway House. ·Oh! how shall I venture or dare
to reveal, &c.*　The first thing to be noticed here is the mis-
naming of the tune "Holloway House" instead of Alloa or
Alloway House, of which there is the account, as follows, in
the annotated *Scots Musical Museum* (Part I., p. 224):—"This
fine melody is the composition of Oswald, and appears in the
first volume of his *Caledonian Pocket Companion*, page 24,
under the title of 'Alloway House.'"　In the original index to
that volume, there is an asterisk (*) prefixed to the name of the
tune, to denote that Oswald was the composer.　The song
[to it] beginning "The Spring returns and clothes the green
plains," was written by the late Reverend Dr. Alexander
Webster, one of the ministers of Edinburgh who projected the
praiseworthy scheme for providing a fund for the Widows of
the Established Clergy of Scotland, which has since been
established with the most beneficial effects.　I have hitherto
been unable to ascertain the locality of this song, as the name
is spelled in two different ways, *Alloway* by the composer of the
air, and *Alloa* by the writer of the song.　Alloway is a parish
in Ayrshire, now of classical celebrity for its having given birth
to Robert Burns, our great national bard.　But Alloa House,
or the Tower of Alloa, which is the scene of Dr. Webster's
song, is situated near a village of the same name in the county
of Clackmanan.　This tower was built about the 13th century,
and was, along with the estate, exchanged by David II. in
1365, with Lord Erskine, progenitor of the Earls of Mar, for
the lands of Stragarthney, in Perthshire.　It is still the favourite
residence of the Erskines of Mar, who are descended of that
ancient and noble family."　Further (p. 307): "Another song
by Dr. Webster, 'Oh! how could I venture to love one like
thee,' also to the same tune, 'Alloa House,' is printed in
The Charmer, vol. i., p. 214, with the signature 'A. W———r.'
It had formerly appeared in the *Scots Magazine* for November,
1747."　It may be added that the tune became a favourite in
England, was sung at Vauxhall (whence doubtless the name
"*Holloway* House") and appeared in many collections.　To

the same tune had been sung Byrom's "Colin and Phœbe," which begins "My time, O ye Muses, was happily spent," which appeared in the *Spectator*, No. 603, 1714.

This song of our *MS.* is given in *Loyal Songs* (1750, p. 35): *Herd* (1776, vol. i., p. 176): Ritson's *Scottish Songs* (p. 272): *Gilchrist* (p. 289). Hogg also printed it in his Second Series of the *Jacobite Relics* (pp. 57-8). He thus annotates:—" Was likewise [as others] copied from Mr. Moir's book of manuscripts, and is rather a commonplace song. The air was set to it at random, being an original air composed by the too little celebrated Mr. Oswald, to whom Scottish music was so much indebted (p. 287)." These various readings from Hogg may interest: st. 1, l. 2, "Too nice for expression"; l. 4, "the" dropped; st. 2, l. 1, "great" for "dear"; l. 2, "great" for "high"; l. 4, "merits" for "merit"; st. 3, l. 1, "But" is dropped and C——n filled in "crown"; l. 3, "deportment" for "behaviour" and "great for "just"; l. 4, "ages" for "Poets"; st. 4, l. 1, "conduct" for "deportment"; l. 2, "divisions" for "division"; l. 4, "And those that now rule shall be glad to obey" for "And those who now rule be compelled to obey." Two stanzas not in the *MS.*, or anywhere else, Hogg, after his manner, doubtless himself composed :—

"May the heavens protect him, and his person rescue,
From the plots and the snares of the dangerous crew;
May they prosper his arms with success in fight,
And restore him again to the crown that's his right.

Then George and his herd shall be banish'd our land,
To his paltry Hanover and German command;
Then freedom and peace shall return to our shore,
And Britons be bless'd with a Stuart once more."

In the *True Loyalist* (as before) there are these verbal changes : st. 1, l. 2, "expression" for "expressing"; st. 4, l. 2, "divisions" for "division."

Pages 1-2. *A Song. From Caledonia's loyal lands.* In st. 1, l. 4, the line is left incomplete in our *MS.* ; but see another version at page 55.

Most of the Jacobite Songs, probably all, were written to 'airs' already wellknown, and with adoption and adaptation of words that were popular. In a very different ['Whig'] *Collection of Loyal Songs, for the Use of the Revolution Club,* Edinburgh, 1749 and 1761 (p. 23), is a Song which should be read in connection with the present. Accordingly I reproduce it :—

Tune—*Over the hills and far away.*

"From barren *Caledonian* lands,
Where rapine uncontroll'd commands,
The rebel clans, in search of prey,
Came o'er the hills and far away.
> *O'er the hills and far away,*
> *O'er the hills and far away ;*
> *The rebel clans, in search of prey,*
> *Came o'er the hills and far away.*

Regardless whether wrong or right,
For booty, not for fame they fight :
Banditti-like they storm, they slay,
They plunder, rob, and run away.
> *O'er the hills,* &c.

With them a vain pretender came,
And perjur'd traitors, dupes to *Rome,*
Resolved all, without delay,
To conquer, die, or run away.
> *O'er the hills,* &c.

Tho' Popish priests among us rule,
Each weak deceiv'd believing fool,
When justice shall her sword display,
She'll drive these locusts far away.
> *O'er the hills,* &c.

Let *Britons,* firm in freedom's cause,
Assist our rights, support our laws,
Defend our faith, our King obey,
And treason soon shall lose its sway,
> *O'er the hills,* &c.

Our sons of war, with martial flame,
Shall bravely merit lasting fame :
Great GEORGE shall *Britain's* sceptre sway,
And chase rebellion far away.
> *O'er the hills,* &c."

This air and refrain was popularized by Gay, Swift and others. St. 2, l. 2, *Duke Billy* is of course William, Duke of Cumberland, on whom see the Introduction. Line 3, *M. Wade* is M[arshall] Wade—on whom also see the Introduction. Line 4, *Sleeping.* There was a sting in this word. It is found in almost all the satires on Sir John Cope, *e.g.*, in the famous ballad of "Johnnie Cope" :—

"Hey, Johnnie Cope, are ye wauking yet?   [*awake*]
Or are ye sleeping, I would wit?   [*know*]
O haste ye, get up, for the drums do beat !
O fie, Cope, rise, in the morning ! "

Hogg, as before (Second Series, pp. 111–113 and 113–115).
On Sir John Cope, see the Introduction in relation to after-
pieces. Lines 5–6, *The Bishops* &c. Cf. the Declaration of
" Prince Charles," pp. 130–140 onward ; also the Letter of
Philalethes to the Archbishop of York, pp. 140–170. Stanza 3,
l. 3, "Great Charles," viz., the Prince Charles Edward, and
" great " is the invariable word of the time.

Page 3.   *The 5th Ode of the 4th Book of Horace immitated.. O Prince,* &c.,
viz., Ad Augustum :—

Divis orte bonis, optime Romulae, etc.

The wonder is that born in Rome as "great Charles " was, the
fact was not more turned to account to catch up and apply
Horatian compliments. The explanation is to be found in the
anxiety to assert the British origin of the Stuarts as against
the (alleged) foreign blood of the House of Hanover. Stanza
2, l. 2, "does" for " dost "—found elsewhere, and frequently in
contemporaries. Similarly, st. 2, l. 3, " are " for " art " ; l. 3,
" James "— not " Charles " yet, so that this is of the earlier
pieces ; st. 7, l, 3—

"The Belgian brutes shall homage pay,
And own our Title to the Sea."

Selden's great work established this 'title.'

,, 4.   *Written in 1747. A Song. As the Devil,* &c. This has a counter-
part in " The Devil o'er Stirling," which begins : "As the
devil o'er Stirling was looking one day," &c. (Hogg, as
before, First Series, pp. 34–36). The odd refrain of " Derry
down, down, down, derry down," belongs to both. Hogg
suspected his ballad "to be of English original " (p. 207).
Stanza 9, l. 1, "Freddy my son " = Frederick, Prince of
Wales ; st. 10, l, 1, " Billy " = William, Duke of Cumberland,
as before. This Song is found variously localized. In
Collection of Loyal Songs (1750, p. 62) is a version differing
verbally here and there, but in no way calling for record, except
that st. 4 thus reads :—

"Oh ! what says the Pope, our Monarch went on ?
And what does he think of my enemy's Son ?
When first I came there his companion reply'd,
I own he had mighty great hopes on his side."

And that st. 6 thus opens :—

"Dejected I heard the sad news I must own,
I thought our affairs would be turn'd upside down;
Were a St———t," &c.

It is oddly headed "The Devil and George Milton," (*sic*—no stop between George and Milton—probably a blind), and to the "Tune, A Cobler there was," &c., in *True Loyalist and Chevalier's Favourite* (1779, p. 93). It may be noted that the corresponding Song, "As the Devil o'er Lincoln was looking one day," written in 1724, is given in Wilkin's *Collection of Political Ballads* (1860, vol. ii., p. 206). As I write this another version appears in *Notes and Queries* (Fifth Series, vol. vi., p. 345).

Page 6. *Nero the Second.* Monstrum horrendum. In full:—"Monstrum horrendum, informe, ingens, cui lumen ademptum" (*Aeneid*, B. III., l. 658). Lines 3-4, "So George . . . . when England's Capital in flames appeared." This "Fire" is unhistorical,—evidently maliciously magnified. Line 24, "Where William struts with patriotic Blood besmear'd." Again the Duke of Cumberland : l. 26, "Turks," seems to have been used as synonymous with the vilest of the vile not = natives of Turkey.

„ 8. *A Speech made by Arthur Lord Balmerino etc.* See on this our Introduction. He was the sixth and last Lord Balmerino : born 1678 : beheaded 18th August, 1746.

„ 9. *Arthurus Dominus de Balmerino Decollatus etc.* Compare with this feminine eulogy the bitter attacks at pages 46-7, 85-6 ; l. 9, "*Pities the Gracefull partner of his fall*": See our Introduction.

„ 10. *Vers Sur le Prince Edüoard.* See our Introduction on these French celebrations of "the Prince." There is a free rendering of part of this at page 89.

„ 15. *The Accomplished Hero* = Prince Charles Edward ; p. 16, l. 9, *Espaliers*=lattice-trained fruit trees; p. 17, l. 5, *King Admetus flocks*: Apollo helped him to secure the "lions & boars" for his chariot, needed to win Alcestis, daughter of Pelias (Eurip. Alcest. 2.); p. 18, l. 5, "begun" for "began" by stress of rhyme; but cf. note on p. 3, st. 2, l. 2.

„ 20. (*The Loyal Resolution*); p. 21, l. 7, *Wiggish* principles=Whiggish; but so spelled throughout, and also "Wigs" for "Whigs"; st. 3, l. 1, *Usurping Nassau*=William III.; l. 5, *Old Noll*= Oliver Cromwell.

„ 22. *The humble address*, &c.; l. 3, *Tories*: on this see our Introduction; l. 12, "lay" for "lie." So late as Byron this Cockneyism prevailed, as in the famous "there let him lay"; l. 19, *spires*—

"spikes" had been a fitter word.   Mr. Hepworth Dixon's
brilliant *History of the Tower* (4 vols. 8vo), fills in the allusions
of the satire.

Page 23.   *A Song.   Would you see three Nations bubled.* "bubled"= cheated,
hum-bugged; st. 3, l. 2, *great James the just* = James II.   This
Song no doubt went to the tune of the Whiggish song written
against James II. before 1688, and which appeared in the first of
the four quarto *Collections of Songs against Popery* issued in
1689 (p. 20).   It must have a place here, as follows:—

" Would you be a Man of Favour?
Would you have your Fortune kind?
Wear the Cross, and eat the Wafer
You'll have all things to your mind.
If the Priest cannot convert you,
Int'rest then must do the thing;
There are Statesmen can inform you,
How to please a Popish King.
Would you see the Papists lowring,
Lost in Horror and affright;
And their Father *Petre* scouring,
Glad of time for happy flight?
Stay but till the *Dutch* are landed,
And the Show will soon appear;
When th' infernal Court's disbanded,
Few will stay for *Tyburn* here."

Nothing could exceed the libellous virulence and scurrility
of the hack-writers employed against the Stuarts.   Another
song, popular at that date, the music to it written by Captain
Packe, was "the Compleat Citizen, or the Man of Fashion":

" Would you be a Man in Fashion?
Would you lead a life divine?
Take a little Dram of Passion,
In a lusty Dose of Wine.
If the Nymph has no Compassion,
Vain it is to sigh and groan;
Love was but put in for Fashion,
Wine will do the Work alone."

This is included among the "180 *Loyal Songs*," 1694, p. 163.
It is also reprinted in *Tixall Poetry*, p. 307.

,, 24.   *The Lamentation*, &c.; st. 3, l. 1, *Brunswick's Strew* = Brunswick;
l. 2, *in Zele* = Zealand? st. 4, l. 3, *Target* = shield or buckler;
st. 8, *Gladsmuir's luckier plain*: see our Introduction on this
battle; st. 14, l. 4, *Sobiesky* = John III., King of Poland, born
1629, died 1696.

Page 27. *The Tears of Scotland.* On this pathetic patriotic lyric by Smollet, see our Introduction for various readings, &c.

„ 29. *The Heroes.* St. 1, l. 4, *Robin*=Robin Hood? St. 2. *Two Dukes.* . . (*a*) "Montague," ll. 1–2. John Montagu succeeded his father Ralph as second Duke of Montagu in 1709, and died 5th July 1749. He married Mary, daughter and co-heir of Marlborough, but his sons all died before him and the title became extinct at his death.

(*b*) "Bolton," *ibid*: Charles Paulet, succeeded his father Charles, as third Duke of Bolton, 21st January, 1721–2, and died 26th August, 1754. He was Constable of the Tower of London. He married first, Anne, only daughter and heir of John, Earl of Carbery; and second, the actress Lavinia Fenton, who had been his mistress. He left no legitimate issue, and his brother Harry succeeded to the title.

(*c*) "Edgecumbe," st. 2, ll. 3–4. Richard Edgecumbe of Mount Edgecumbe, in the county of Devon, became a Lord of the Treasury in 1716, and was created Baron Edgecumbe 20th April, 1742. In 1743 he became Chancellor of the Duchy of Lancaster. His second son, George, who succeeded as third Baron, was created Earl of Mount Edgecumbe.

4. "Herbert," *ibid*: Henry-Arthur Herbert, son of Richard Herbert, by Florence, sister and co-heir of Edward and Henry, third and fourth Lords Herbert of Chirbury of the first creation; becoming heir male to that family, was created Baron Herbert of Chirbury, 21st December, 1743; and Earl of Powis, 27th May, 1748. He died in 1772.

„ 30, st. 4, l. 4, "Russel." There was no "Lord Russell" in 1745–50. John Russell, fourth Duke of Bedford, succeeded to the title in 1732, and died in 1771; and his only son was not born until 1739. Probably the Duke of Bedford was meant.

„ 30, st. 5, l. 4, "Granby": John Manners, commonly called Marquis of Granby, was eldest son of John, third duke of Rutland. He was born in 1721, and died in 1770 before his father. He was the distinguished Commander-in-Chief, and as such figures still on many an Inn's sign-board. His son Charles succeeded as fourth Duke of Rutland. *Ibid*, l. 8, *Charles of Sweden*: viz., Charles X. Gustavus, born 1622, died February 13th, 1660.

„ 31, st. 6, l. 1, "Harcourt": Simon Harcourt, succeeded his grand-father Simon in 1727, as second Viscount Harcourt, and was created Earl of Harcourt in 1749. He was Viceroy of Ireland in 1772. He died 16th September 1777. The title expired on the death of his second son in 1830. *Ibid, Halifax*: George Montagu succeeded his father George, as second Earl of Halifax, in 1739, and died in 1772, leaving no male issue, when the title became

extinct. He was First Lord of the Admiralty, Lord Lieutenant
of Ireland (in 1749), and Secretary of State. *Ibid, Falmouth*:
Hugh Boscawen succeeded his father Hugh, as second Vis-
count Falmouth, in 1734. He was a general officer in the
Army and Captain of the Yeomen of the Guard. He died 4th
March, 1782, without issue. *Ibid*, l. 6, *Cholmondeley*: George
Cholmondeley succeeded his father George, as third Earl
Cholmondeley in 1733, and died in 1770. He married Mary,
only daughter of Sir Robert Walpole, first Earl of Oxford.
Ibid, Earl Berkley: John Berkeley succeeded his father Wil-
liam, as fifth Baron Berkeley of Stratton in 1740, and died in
1773, without issue, when the title became extinct. He was
Captain of the Band of Gentlemen Pensioners in 1746, and
subsequently Constable of the Tower of London.

Page 31, st. 7, l. 1, *Gower*: John Leveson Gower succeeded his father Sir
John as second Baron Gower in 1709, and was created Earl
Gower 8th July, 1746. He died 25th December, 1754. He
was ancestor of the present Duke of Sutherland.

,, 32. *U. D.* On these letters see Introduction; l. 19, *William*=Duke of
Cumberland; l. 33, *A Youth*=the Prince Charles Edward;
p. 33, l. 25, *gaue his father Birth*: I suppose=fore-father, for
certes James was not born in Scotland; p. 34, l. 25, *Zenophon*
=Xenophon; p. 35, l. 5, *Seaton*: George Seton, tenth Lord
Seton and fifth Earl of Winton, who joined the Rising of 1715,
was taken prisoner at Preston, attainted and left for execution.
He contrived, however, to escape from the Tower of London
in 1716 and fled to France, and finally to Rome, where he died
19th December, 1749; *ibid*, l. 6, *Falkirk* . . . . . . *Hawley*: In
The Genealogist (No. 4, April, 1876) is a paper entitled,
"Does an Heir to the Barony of Hawley exist"? (pp. 161–165).
I don't concern myself greatly as to the "Heir," but there are
certain tid-bits on our "hero" worth transferring here, as thus—
"Lieutenant-General Henry Hawley, who was Colonel of the
first (Royal) Dragoons, Governor of Portsmouth, and Aide-de-
Camp to the King, left no legitimate children. He held a command in Scotland during the Rebellion of 1745–46, and seems
to have acquired some property in that kingdom, as, after his
death, which occurred at his seat near Portsmouth, 23rd March,
1759, when he was above eighty, his sister Miss Anne Hawley,
then resident in London, was served heir general to him
18th March, 1762. This service alone is sufficient to upset any
claim to legitimate descent from General Hawley, but fortu-
nately his Will is conclusive on this point, and moreover shews
the origin of the Toovey-Hawley family. It is dated 29th
March, 1749 (with four codicils), and is a most curious

document. He directs that his funeral be conducted like that of a common soldier from the hospital, many of whom are as good men as himself; that the carpenter be paid for the "carcase box"; that if the priest demand a fee, "let the puppy have it," and so on. He leaves his whole fortune in certain proportions to his only sister Anne, to Captain William Toovey and Lieutenant-Colonel John Toovey, both of his own regiment, sons of Mrs. Elizabeth Toovey, widow, who is to life-rent most of what Captain Toovey succeeds to, and who had been, "for many years his friend & companion, often his careful nurse, and in his absence, a faithful steward." There is also a bequest to Elizabeth Burkett spinster, niece to Mrs. Toovey, who is descibed as having been "a useful handmaid" to him. The Will proceeds, "As I never was married, I have no heirs; I therefore have long since taken it into my head to adopt one heir & son after the manner of the Romans." He goes on to place Captain William Toovey in this position, makes him his sole executor, and instructs him to take both his names. The legacy to Elizabeth Burkett is left on condition that she never marries Colonel Toovey, "and if he is fool enough to marry her," then all provisions in their favour are to become null, and Miss Hawley is given power to proceed against them and recover their shares of his estate. The parentage of General Hawley seems unknown: an absurd statement has appeared that he was an illegitimate son of George II., who was four or five years his junior; l. 11, *Alva* = the infamous Spanish general; p. 36, l. 7, *So judg'd* (see 1 *Kings*, iii).

Page 37. *A Birth Day Ode*, viz., of Prince Charles Edward. I take the following note on the poem from *Jacobite Minstrelsy* (Glasgow, 1828-9): "The original manuscript of this composition, which was only published a few years ago, remained for three-fourths of a century in the possession of a distinguished family in Somersetshire, to whose Jacobite ancestor it had been presented by its author, the Rev. Dr. Isaacs, of Exeter. The care with which it was thus preserved as a literary relic, shews that the principles which it inculcates, and for which the West of England was notorious in 1715, were not by any means extinct there in 1745." (p. 322). Our *MS.* is dated 1747; Dr. Isaac's, 1746. Stanza 1, l. 4, *Turn from the Ax*, &c.: To the same source I am indebted for the following hereon : "This allusion denotes that the scaffold had recently exhibited the last scene of the tragedy which followed the government victory at Culloden. The massacre and devastation perpetrated by the Duke of Cumberland in the Highlands, was not deemed punishment enough for the vanquished Jacobites. It was thought necessary, also, to strike terror in the south as well as in the north ; and accordingly, a long list of those who had been taken prisoners, or who had delivered themselves up, was made out for prosecution, under the statutes against High Treason. Several hundreds were arraigned at London, York, and Carlisle, and out of the numerous convictions obtained, about eighty suffered death at the hands of the executioner. All these unfortunate individuals are said to have met their fate with heroic fortitude and resolution ; and some of them even gloried in their political martyrdom in such a manner as to astonish the beholders. With one exception also they continued to the last to justify the cause which had brought them to the scaffold, praying for the exiled Royal Family, and particularly for Prince Charles, whom they represented as a pattern of excellency, and qualified to make the nation happy, should it ever have the good fortune to see him restored." (pp. 322–3.)

Page 41. *An Ode.* "—redeunt Saturnia regna " : = Ec. iv, 6.

,, 43. *Tho' the ungodly*, &c. Line 2, "Jacob's " = Jacobus, James; p. 44, l. 6, *Welcom'd . . . . . . with op'ning skies* ; a somewhat profane reference to *St. Mark*, i. 10. The author of these Lines was Alexander Robertson, of Strowan, in whose Poems they are found. Our *MS.* has superior readings. The following from the " Poems" may be noted : p. 43, l. 1, "rebellious" for "ungodly ; l. 2, " rightful " for " righteous " ; l. 5, "with . . . . . army" for "their . . . . . force"; l. 9, "God" for "Heaven"; l. 12, "views" for "weighs " and "finds them still," and—

> " Unable to perform his sacred Will ;
> Do thou implore him in the Hours of Need
> He'll sink the Proud, and make the Stubborn bleed ;

p. 44, l. 3, "Those . . . . . . times" for "Those . . . . . . days"; l. 6, "a" for "as" and "by" for "with " ; l. 9, "saving" for "loving"; l. 11, "expanded" for "extended"; l. 12, sphere" for "sky"; l. 13, "thy" for "the " and "disperse " for "dispell ; l. 15, "is" for "in" (*his*); l. 17, "then" for "than" and "stars" for "Suns" and "but faintly can express " for "but faint express"; last line, "loudest" for "awful" ; p. 45, l. 4, "confederated " for "confederate"; l. 7, "insult " for "invade"; l. 14, "fix'd upon" for "settled on." There are also transpositions of lines. It is headed "The 20th Psalm imitated from Buchanan."

,, 45. *If you the Paths*, &c. ; p. 46, l. 5. *The Glorious Nine* : one of many such groups executed in that bloody time ; l. 7, *th' intrepid Three*, Balmerino, Kilmarnock, and Cromarty ; but the last was pardoned; l. 25, *Cromartie*: George Mackenzie succeeded his father John as third Earl of Cromarty in 1731. He was attainted and condemned to death for his part in the Rising of 1745, but his life was spared, and the attainder finally reversed in behalf of his son, John Lord Macleod; p. 47, l. 17, *martyr'd Charles* = Charles I.

Page 48. *The* 137*th Psalm*. Stanza 2, l. 4, *Batavian Strand* = Holland; st. 6, l. 2, *Drummosie* = Culloden, as in the touching fragment preserved if not composed by Burns. The brother of "Mʳ Wᵐ Hamilton" to whom this "Imitation" is assigned, was John Hamilton, who was the elder brother of the "sweet Singer" of "The Braes of Yarrow." He died unmarried at Ninewar, in East Lothian, on 8th May, 1570, when the family estate descended to William Hamilton; st. 7, *Faithless freind*: See Introduction, on France.

,, 49. *A Soliloquy*. The heading of the "Soliloquy" is important as establishing the hitherto unverified statement in Burke's *Landed Gentry* (*s.n.*) that he "was present at the battle of Culloden." The last editor of the *Poems and Songs* of Hamilton (i vol., 1850), James Paterson, says: "It is uncertain whether Hamilton took any active part in the rebellion. He was probably prevented from doing so, as Mr. James Chalmers supposes, by the illness of his wife, to whom he was much attached, and who died in 1745." (p. xxxi). Referring to Burke (as *supra*) he continues: "As there are several obvious blunders in the article, little reliance is to be placed upon it . . . . Be the fact as it may, however, his Jacobite hopes were completely extinguished by the decisive victory of Culloden; and he was constrained to consult his safety in flight, lurking for several months in the Highlands, where he suffered much, both physically and mentally." (p. xxxii). The "Soliloquy" appeared anonymously in the *Scots Magazine* for June, 1746. It has been reprinted in all the editions of Hamilton's Poems. Page 50, l. 6, omits this couplet :—

> "Lest, hapless victors in the mortal strife,
> Through death we struggle but to second life."

On the other hand, p. 50, ll. 13-14 of our *MS.* do not appear in any of the editions; l. 19 reads "horror" for "honor"; and p. 50, last line, "Pleas'd with thy lot."

,, 52. *On Sᵗ Andrew's day* 1746. Throughout it looks like "Sʳ Andrew." This is a stupid piece of attempted blank verse by some one who knew not its laws. Nor is the hazy thought less imperfect than the workmanship. Who "Macduff" on l. 4 was, it is now impossible to say.

Page 55.　*A Song. From Caledonia's Loyal Lands.* In st. 1, l. 4, I have
printed "Honour's" for the nonsensical word in the *MS.*,
"Hanowis," albeit somewhat tautological. Cf. the poem
earlier in our *M.S.*, at pp. 1-2.

„　56.　*A Song, made in the Year* 1745. Hogg has this note on the refrain, "Up
and war 'em a' Willy":—"There not being a Willie of any
note in the whole Jacobite army, the chorus must have been an
older one, adapted, not improbably, from a song of King William's
time" (2nd Series, as before, pp. 256-7: Song V., "When we
went to the field of war," &c.). *Scotice,* "war" is spelled
"waur." St. 1, l. 7, "'em" is English, not Scottish; st. 2,
l. 1, "nea" is Cockney for the Scottish "nae"=no; l. 3,
Lochiell=Lochiel—the Scottish "h" too much for an
Englishman; st. 3, l. 4, *lards,* again the Cockney for
"lairds"—landowners (of Skye); st. 4, l. 3, *Appen Keppock* (=Keppoch), and *Clanronald*—all familiar names of the
period; st. 5, l. 5, *Glymores*=claymores—no Scotchman
could have so (mis)spelled: in the museum at Southport
Botanic Gardens I read the other day, on a rusted specimen
of an ancient "claymore," the word "glaymire" as its name!
st. 6, l. 3, *Perth,* see before; st. 7, l. 3, *Brave Lord
George, or rather Traitor,* see all the "Histories" on this,
also on l. 4, *Nairn and Cask*; st. 9, l. 7, *Ick,* an odd
spelling of "ilk," Scotice "each"—an Englishman's mistake;
st. 10, l. 3, *hen'a* = binna, be not; st. 12, l. 1, *Sir John
Cope,* see our Introduction; l. 3, *to the Cross*—Robert
Fergusson repeatedly celebrates this historic monument in his
raciest poems, and everybody knows how effectively Scott has
introduced it into Novel and Poem; st. 13, l. 1, *hug,* an
impossible word from a Scotchman here; st. 15, l. 4, *sea*
for "sae," *i.e.* so—like "nea" for "nae," betrays the Englishman, not Scotchman; l. 5, *Glimores,* see as st. 5, l. 5; st.
16, l. 5, *en* for "an' a'"=if all—again English, not Scotch;
st. 17, l. 1, *Lascelles,* frequently named in the history of the
period; l. 5, *Mun*=man—one more such impossible Scotch
as still appears in *Punch* and other Cockney publications; st.
18, l. 1, *Wady* = Marshal Wade, as before; l. 6, *mucle* =
muckle or mickle—much.

„　62.　*A Song. Tune, When Britons first &c.* This appears in *Jacobite
Minstrelsy,* as before, and I transfer here its full note on it, as
thus :—"Notwithstanding the disastrous termination of Prince
Charles' expedition in 1746, the Jacobite muse despaired not
of the cause of his family, nor ceased to hope, as expressed in
the effusions of loyalty and zeal, that the time was not far distant when he should once more

" Return triumphant o'er his foes,
    And ruling Britain, end their woes."
The reception which Charles met with at the Court of France
after effecting his escape, and the liberality of the French
government in protecting the exiles who followed in his train,
afforded, among other circumstances, a strong ground for in-
dulging in such hopes. No sooner was it understood at Versailles that His Royal Highness had landed at a French port,
than the castle of St. Anthonie was prepared for his reception;
and a cavalcade of young noblemen was appointed to meet and
congratulate him on his safe return. The fame of his exploits
in Scotland had already preceded him, and on the Court, as
well as on the French people, had made such an impression as
rendered him everywhere an object of interest and curiosity.
When he arrived at Versailles, the King was attending a
Council of his Ministers, but his Majesty instantly rose and
went out to welcome him. 'My dearest Prince,' said he,
tenderly embracing him, 'I thank Heaven for thus seeing
you returned in safety, after so many fatigues and dangers;
you have proved yourself possessed of all the qualities of the
heroes and philosophers of antiquity, and I hope you will one
day receive the reward of such extraordinary merit.' After
spending some time with the King, Charles passed to the
apartment of the Queen, who received him with the same
demonstrations of respect and affection. And when he was
about to withdraw from the palace, the whole Court crowded
around him to express their admiration of his heroic enterprise,
and the satisfaction with which they saw him once more in
France. Every where did he receive similar testimonies of
congratulation and esteem, and this gallant nation, so prone to
admire whatever is great, enterprising, and heroic in the actions
of men, almost beheld realised in the person of Charles, the
beau ideal of Chivalry, a real *preux Chevalier*, who in their
enthusiasm they likened to their own celebrated Bayard, *sans
peur et sans reproche.*" (pp. 350, 351.) On the obverse of the
medal, see all the Histories and these Notes. The Tune
of this Song, it is to be noted, belongs to Thomson's
"When Britain first at Heaven's command," &c., with its
proud chorus of "Britannia rules the waves." This famous Song
first appeared in the *Masque of Alfred* in 1740. The *Masque*
was written, jointly, by Thomson, author of *The Seasons*, and
Castle of Indolene; and David Mallet, author of *William &*
Margaret, and *Edwin & Emma*. In the *Masque*, as altered
by Mallet in 1751, three of the six original stanzas were omitted,
and three additional stanzas, written by Lord Bolingbroke, were

substituted. Dr. Dimsdale, in his *Ballads and Songs* by David Mallet (1857), claims "Rule Britannia" for Mallet; but his argument rests on statements by Mallet, and *he* is never to be believed. For my part, I must hold Thomson to have written it.

It may be well to add, that "Rule Britannia" is printed on p. 6 of "A Collection of Loyal Songs," for the use of the Revolution Club. Some of which never before printed. Edinburgh, printed by Robert Fleming, 1749, reprinted 1761. It also appeared in "A Collection of Loyal Songs, Poems," &c., 1750. Ritson mentions having heard a few lines of a fine parody of *Rule Britannia*, of which he could never obtain a copy. The chorus ran thus:

> " Rise, Britannia, Britannia, rise & fight;
> Restore your injur'd monarch's right."
> (*Scotish Songs*, 1794, vol. i, p. lxix.

It is as a Jacobite song he mentions this. Southey observes, "The song of *Rule Britannia* . . . . . . will be the political hymn of the country as long as she maintains her political power." (*Later English Poets*, vol. ii, p. 107.) St. 3, l. 6, *G——* is of course "George." It was the mode thus to guise treason; and so with "crown" as *C——*, "King" as *K——*, "Hanover" as *H——* and the like.

Page 62. Heading. There is no difficulty in filling in these initials, 'viz., To his R[oyal] H[ighness] C[harles] P[rince] of W[ales] R[egent] of the K[ingdoms] of G[reat] B[ritain] F[rance] and I[reland]. l. 13, *artless* = unskilful; p. 63, l. 21, *Vasa* = Gustavus de Vasa; p. 64, l. 8, *Glencoe*: the head of the House of Clanranald or The Macdonalds; l. 20, *Cameron*: This was Donald Cameron of Lochiel, named "Young Lochiel" from his father being still living. He earned the further name of the "gentle Lochiel" and stands second only to his illustrious grandfather, Sir Ewen Cameron. He shared all the "wanderings" of Prince Charles Edward, and escaped with him to France. He died in 1748. P. 66, l. 4, *Sobieski*: See note on page 24, st. 4, l. 4 ; l. 23, *the gracious declaration* : See it pp. 130-140 : p. 67, l. 5, *Glengary, Keppoch* [= Keppoch, *i.e.* the head of the Keppoch Macdonalds], *Appin* [*i.e.* the Stuarts] : l. 11, *Glenbucket, i.e.*, Stewart of Glenbuckie: These are well known "chiefs" or "lairds" (= landed proprietors) or other prominent representatives of the Princes' adherents in the Scottish Highlands. They come up in every History of the Rebellions. It were superfluous pains to annotate them further here. l. 17, *Athol's Duke*: This was William, second son of

the second marquis and first Duke of Athol, who acted very
prominently in both the Scottish Rebellions. He was one
of the first to join the Earl of Mar in 1715. In 1745, he
accompanied Prince Charles Edward from exile in France into
Scotland, and landed with him at Borodale 25th July. He was
styled Duke of Athol by the Jacobites, though his attainder
transferred the family honours to a younger brother. He died
in the Tower of London on 9th July, 1746. l. 19, *T——t*:
qu. = Tyrant? p. 68, l. 7, *Murray*: viz., Lord George Murray,
commander-in-chief of Prince Charles's army. He was fourth
son of the first Duke of Athol. He died in Holland on 8th
July, 1760, leaving a great historic fame. l. 16, *Perth*: James,
Lord Drummond, Duke of Perth, joined Prince Charles Edward
on his arrived at Perth, in September, 1745. He saw much
service in the Rebellion. He fled after Culloden and embarked
for France, but being quite exhausted with the fatigues he had
undergone, died on the passage 11th May, 1746, having just
completed his thirty-third year. l. 22, *Ogilvie*: This no doubt,
was Lord Ogilvie, son of the Earl of Airlie, though another, viz.,
Captain Ogilvy, son of Sir David Ogilvy (second baronet), is still
more famous earlier. He was with King James II. at the
Boyne, and to him is ascribed the Jacobite song,

> " It was a' for our rightful King
>   We left fair Scotland's strand."

He was one of the hundred gentlemen who volunteered to attend
their royal master in exile and fell in an engagement on the
Rhine. P. 69, l. 1, *Nairn*: The Honourable Robert Nairne,
second son of Lord William Murray, second Lord Nairne. He
fell at Culloden, 16th April, 1746. It is from this line descended the Baroness Nairn, whose many pathetic and also
humorous Scotish songs have given a new lease of renown to
the name. *Gask, i.e.,* Oliphant of Gask, as in note *supra* on
p. 67, l. 5; p. 69, l. 7, *Strowan* = Struan, *i.e.,* Robertson of
Strowan, the (so-called) Poet—heir of an illustrious line. His
life covers the History of Scotland for the period, so prominent
and potential was he. After all its stormfulness, he died in his
own house of Carie, in Rannoch, April 18th, 1749, in his eighty-
first year. He was the prototype of the Baron of Bradwardine,
in *Waverley.* l. 11, *Menzies*: Probably Menzies of Culdares,
who, having been pardoned for his share in the rebellion of 1715,
felt himself bound not to join in that of 1745, although he sent
a gift of a horse to the Prince. Or it may have been Menzies
of Shian, who, in 1745, called out the clan. l. 15, *Grahams*:
A full and most interesting account of this many-branched

Family, will be found in William Andrews' *Scotish Nation* (3 vols. 8vo, *s.n.*); l. 21, *From Perth*: This was an epoch-march in the Rebellion of 1745. The following poem, from *Loyal Poems* (1750, p. 127), is an interesting parallel. It has been so utterly overlooked in common with all our quotations, &c., from the volume, as to be almost equally valuable with manuscript.

A POEM.

" On P——ce C——s's Victory at Gl——muir.

Hail, happy Scotland! bless the long'd-for day,
That shines propitious with a chearful ray;
See from her bed thine ancient honour springs,
She lifts her crest, and claps her joyful wings.
No more shall ease her splendid form obscure,
The scornful victim of a foreign pow'r—
Thy warlike sons, a brave and gen'rous band,
Contend for freedom, to their native land!
And what bold hand to check their course shall dare,
While godlike C——s commands the glorious war?
In vain rebellion shakes his pointless dart,
To damp the valour of his dauntless heart,
Firm as a rock he'll stem the raging tide,
'Till in full triumph He victorious ride.
But now small space the diff'rent hosts divide,
The scheme is laid on brave M⁰Donal'ds side,
Night draws her curtains, ere the battle joins,
The rebel-army fires their outmost lines.
Not so the Clans, but in soft slumbers laid,—
They wait the morning in their tartan plaid.
First starts the P——ce, ere Phœbus shed one ray,
And bless'd the dawning of th' important day.
O heav'ns! he said, while heav'n attentive heard,
This day may justice have its due reward,
If what I ask, if what I seek be mine,
On me may your indulgent favour shine;
But if I am to gain another's right,
May all my forces here be put to flight;
Amen, he cries. The army hears around,
And springs like light'ning from the humid ground.
Abash'd, they view their P——ce, and smote their breast,
That he should rise ere they could leave their rest.
But soon compos'd they lend an anxious ear,
And list'ning, lean his gracious words to hear.

"My friends, (he says, and draws his flaming sword,)
I trust my person to your sacred word;
Like you unmail'd, ye view me here all o'er,
The first in danger, as the first in pow'r:
This day I hope thro' God Almighty's aid,
Ye shall a free and happy race be made.
Pursue my steps, I'll lead a warlike van,
And should heav'n frown, I'll fall the destin'd man;
Yet may that heav'n be all their sure defence,
Who fight in favour of their injur'd P——ce.
But if good success crown our dawning hope,
And we gain conquest o'er rebellious C——pe.
This is my will, this is my high behest,
In hopes for once you'll grant your P——ce request.
Car——lus Rex, the word; let you and I,
Or conquer here, or bravely die."

The Editor of *Loyal Poems*, in printing the preceding, intimates that it had reached him in a very corrupt state, and that he had been obliged to revise it. He laments that he was ignorant of "the gentleman to whom the world is obliged for this excellent piece," and thus concludes:—"If it ever happens that a Copy of this should fall into the Hands of the worthy Author, the Publishers flatter themselves He will readily forgive their Presumption when He considers the Occasion of it; & are not without Hopes, that this may induce Him to do Himself Justice, and to give a more perfect Pleasure to the World, by an Edition of this Poem, published under His own Eye and as Himself wrote it."

Page 72. *To Mr J. M. on his turning Evidence.* This was John Murray of Broughton who was Secretary to Prince Charles. He became Sir John Murray of Broughton, Bart. He died 6th December, 1777.

,, 75. *If heaven is pleas'd,* &c. This has been frequently printed.

,, 77. *A Song.* *Britons who dare to claim,* &c. This was published by Hogg (as before, 2nd series, pp. 52-3) and as it follows the King's Anthem (applied to Prince Charles) he annotates "Is *another of the same,* like old Mr. Johnson's psalm" (p. 286.)—whatever that may have been. St. 5, ll. 1-3—

Down with Dutch Politicks,
Wigs, knaves, & fanaticks,
The old Rump's cause.

on which *Jacobite Minstrelsy* annotates—"This seems a shrewd alllusion to the policy of William in keeping fair with his English subjccts, while he was advancing the interests of his friends in Holland. The Rump Parliament, in Cromwell's time, is perfectly understood " (p. 148). This Song previous to Hogg appeared in *Loyal Songs* (1750, p. 62) and *True Loyalist, or Chevalier's Favourite* (1779, p. 62). The variations are trivial. Chappell also gives it in his *Popular Music of the Olden Time*, p. 705.

Page 78. *A Song. Thou Butcher of the Northern Clime* = the Duke of Cumberland at Culloden and in the North generally. This is found in *Loyal Songs* (1750, p. 47).

,, 79. *A Song. Made in 1746.* Appeared in *Loyal Songs* (as before, p. 54) to the tune of "The Widow can bake and the Widow can brew." The variations are of no importance. But here is another to the same tune and from the same source (pp. 58-9):—

> " Let Sol curb his Coursers, and stretch out the Day,
> That Time may not hinder Carouzing and Play,
> That we may be chearful, and all nature gay,
> Upon the Birth-day of our Laddie.
> > *With the Down of a Thistle we'll make him a Bed,*
> > *With Roses and Lillies we'll pillow his Head,*
> > *And with a tun'd Harp we'll gently aid,*
> > *To ease in soft slumbers our Laddie.*
>
> Our Laddie can fight, and our Laddie can sing,
> He's fierce as the North Wind, and blythe as the Spring.
> And his Soul was design'd for no less than a King,
> Such Virtues appear in our Laddie.
> > *With the Down,* &c.
>
> Let Thunderbolts rattle o'er Mountains of Snow,
> And Hurricanes over cold Caucasus blow ;
> Let Care be confin'd to the Regions below,
> When we have got home our bright Laddie.
> > *With the Down,* &c.
>
> Then through the fair Forest, he'll chace the wild Bull,
> And tear the Horns off from his G—n thick Skull ;
> For he wou'd destroy, had he but his Will,
> Our Friends, and their bonny bright Laddie.
> > *With the Down,* &c.
>
> Then open our Cellars, and deal out the Wine,
> And let us carouze it 'till our Noses shine ;
> And curse on the Wretch that wou'd seem to decline,
> The drinking Success to our Laddie.
> > *With the Down,* &c.''

Page 82. *Townley's Ghost.* See on this our Introduction, and in the large paper *fac-simile* of the whole of it.

,, 84. *Verses addressed to the Pretended Duke of Cumberland on seeing him represented in the Print of the Battle of Culloden,* &c. ; *Ibid, other Verses,* &c. See note on page 9.

,, 85. *A Song. What's the Spring, breathing Jessamine,* &c. This appears in Hogg (First Series, p. 126), and in *Jacobite Minstrelsy* (as before, p. 362). Both misprint "Spring-breathing" for "Spring, breathing," in correspondence with Summer and Autumn. Hogg annotates : "Is a beautiful song, to the old Scotch air of *Tweedside*" (p. 291). Prior to Hogg, this is given in *Loyal Songs* (as before, p. 51), and in *The Masque* (1767, p. 252). In the former (besides verbal variations of no moment) in st. 3, ll. 1, 3, read :—

> "No Sweetness the Senses can share
> . . . .
> No brightness that Gloom e'er can cheer."

In st. 5, ll. 3–4, thus run :—

> "The Rights they defended, and those
> They bought with their Blood we'll ne'er Sell."

,, 86. *Verses wrote by a Lady on seeing the Picture of the Prince.* This was probably the celebrated portrait by Le Tocque, painted at Paris in 1748, which became a popular "print" among the Jacobites. It certainly answers to the fervent laudation of "*Bonnie* Prince Charlie." It has been re-engraved by Freeman.

,, 87. *England's Prayers :* l. 2, *Our Church* = the Church of Rome ? l. 3, *Turks,* see note on p. 6, l. 26.

,, 89. *Verses occasioned by the late thanksgiving day* : For (I suppose) the "famous victory" of Culloden.

,, 89. *On the French seizing the Prince and conducting him prisoner out of Paris :* See the original French at pp. 10-15. Line 5, *Fontenoy* : Fought 30th April (11th May, N.S.), 1745, between the French, commanded by Saxe, and the English, Hanoverians, Dutch, and Austrians, commanded by the Duke of Cumberland. Line 7, *St. Severin* : St. Severin's day is October 23rd. One so named was Archbishop of Cologne, A.D. 400; another (St. Severin of Turin) was patron of Bordeaux. See *Hone's Every Day Book,* 1825 ; vol. i, cols. 1393-4 ; vol. ii, cols. 1350-52. Line 11, *To place a Woman on the Imperial throne :* Who could be meant? I don't hazard a guess. Line 16, *B——s* = Britain's. Line 18, *Most Christian King* = Louis XVI. I give the continuation here of the note from *Jacobite Minstrelsy* on p. 62, as it very well illustrates the indignation of the present poem and the others in like strain :—" In addition to the personal regard thus testified for Prince Charles by Louis XV. and his people, it was officially stated, that a new expedition would soon be fitted out, and composed of such an effective force as would enable him to overcome all opposition. Accordingly several regiments of the exiled cavaliers were embodied immediately, at the head of which were placed Lochiel, Lord Ogilvie, and some others who had distinguished themselves in the late insurrection. These levies were posted at Dieppe, Boulogne, and Calais, and they served for a while as demonstrations of a serious intention to effect another invasion. Subsequent events, however, demonstrate that the French Court were never serious in their intention; and finally, the Prince & his partizans found that they & their cause were but as dust in the balance, when weighed against the policy which dictated that both should be sacrificed to the political interests of France. In 1748, negotiations for peace, which had been entered into with the British government a year before, were brought to a close, and the treaty of Aix-la-Chapelle was soon after made public. According to one of its provisions, France not only acknowledged the right of the House of Hanover to the Crown of England, but agreed that, in terms of a treaty entered into in 1718, she should utterly renounce all alliance with the Pretender and his family, and cease to permit them to reside within her territory. Thus at one & the same time, did the Scottish Jacobites discover the hollow and deceitful character of the promised assistance of the French King, and the hopes of the unfortunate Charles Edward were extinguished for ever.

"Notwithstanding the express stipulation in this treaty, that the Stuarts should be deprived of the rights of hospitality in France, Prince Charles lingered in that country for a considerable time, vainly imagining, that national policy would yield to the point of honour in the breast of the French King, who had pledged himself to see the Stuart family restored. At length the ministry gave Charles unequivocal proofs of their determination to fulfil this condition of the treaty ; and it was plainly intimated to him, that if he did not withdraw himself from France, he would be conveyed out of it by force. Charles only replied, that all he wanted, was 'that the King should keep his word'; and he continued to go about Paris, attending the opera and all public places as usual. A petty official warfare ensued in messages and counter-messages, which, however ridiculous in itself, created a great sensation in the frivolous Court of Louis XV. For a person in Charles's circumstances to attempt to thwart the government of the Grand Monarque, was in those days deemed a very extraordinary instance of daring, and caused him accordingly to become, as it were, an object of national interest. Previously the people had looked upon him as a being of superior order, in consequence of the wild and romantic character of his Scottish expedition ; but now their admiration was still more increased, because they considered him a martyr to political expediency, and suffering under unmerited misfortunes. Whenever, therefore, he appeared in public, the people crowded after him ; and when he entered the theatres or other places of amusement, he became the sole object of interest & attention. ' On such occasions,' says a contemporary, ' he himself seemed the only person indifferent to his fate. He talked with good humour and gaiety upon every other topic of the day, to the young noblemen who surrounded him, but no one could speak to him without mingled emotions of admiration and respect, and few beheld him without tears.' This state of things, however, could not be permitted to last, if the ministry meant to preserve the faith of a public treaty. Besides, it was now perceptible that the public feeling so strongly excited in Charles's favour, was by no means agreeable to the French King. And, to add to the embarrassment, the Earl of Sussex and Lord Cathcart, then residing in Paris, as hostages to guarantee fulfilment of certain parts of the late treaty, complained bitterly of the marked respect everywhere shown to the public enemy of their country, while they were treated with ill-suppressed contempt or dislike. Louis, therefore, addressed a letter to Charles's father at Rome, demanding that he should be withdrawn by parental authority from the French territory, otherwise active measures would be resorted to, in order to compel his departure.

" The Old Chevalier instantly obeyed this mandate, and by letter commanded the Prince to fulfil the King's wishes Charles, however, though said to have always entertained the utmost respect for his father, in this case remained inflexible, and held out obstinately against his command. He stated that he still looked to the honour of Louis for a fulfilment of all his engagements, and declared in the most peremptory manner that no pensions, promises or advantages whatever, should induce him to renounce his just rights ; but, on the contrary, that he was resolved to consecrate the last moment of his life to their recovery. The French ministers in this dilemma, advised their monarch to call a Council of State ; which was accordingly held, and there it was at last determined to end

the difficulty by sending the Prince out of the kingdom by
force. Louis, it would appear, only yielded to this measure
from a conviction of its political necessity, for he was known to
entertain a warm affection for his unfortunate guest; and when
the order of arrest was presented to him for signature, he exclaimed, with unaffected regret, '*Ah pauvre Prince, qu'il est
difficile pour un roi d'etre un veritable ami'!* The order was
immediately put in execution, and Charles was conducted to
the Castle of Vincennes, where, in a small apartment, attended
only by one real friend, the faithful Neil MacEachan, who, with
Flora Macdonald, had accompanied him on his journey through
Skye, he was left to ruminate on his wayward fortunes. The
unhappy Prince had borne himself with dignity and composure
at the moment of his being taken into custody; and while the
military escort was conveying him to Vincennes, he spoke in a
haughty tone, as if to prove that he scorned the treatment he
experienced; but according to MacEachan's report, no sooner
had the officers retired, than he clasped his hands together, and
burst into tears, exclaiming, 'Ah, my faithful Highlanders!
you would never have treated me thus—would I were still
among you!'" (pp. 351–3).

Page 91. *The Landlord A Song. 1715.* This appeared in *Loyal Songs* (as
before, pp. 56, 58). The tune, " When young at the Bar," &c.,
which is that of a Song in the *Beggars Opera.* The initial
stanza may serve as a specimen of the variations from our *MS.*:—

" What ails thee, poor Shepherd, why looks thee so wan,
So meagre thy Face, and so ghastly thy Mein;
Has any Distemper infected thy Sheep?
Or does lovely Phillis disturb thy sweet sleep?
That thou should'st sit here by the Shades, and complain;
What is it perplexes and troubles thy brain?"

Our st. 3, l. 5, commences the stanza and reads better, "So
dull are my Notes, on my Pipe I can't play," &c., and our l. 3
is l. 5, and for "French" has "Germany."
The closing stanza opens thus:

" Chear up, honest Shepherd, and calm thy grieved Heart,
Gird thy sword by thy Side, act a true British Part."

—spirited, but without the stinging sarcasm, "like a true English priest." With reference to the tune, "When young at the
bar" (*supra*), it belonged to Lucy Lockit's song in the *Beggars
Opera* (1727), act iii, as thus:—

" When young at the bar you first taught me to score,
And bid me be free of my lips and no more;

I was kiss'd by the Parson, the Squire, and the Sot,
When the guest was departed, the kiss was forgot;
But *his* kiss was so sweet, and so closely he prest,
That I languish'd and pin'd, till I granted the rest."
This is the same tune as Baildon's music to Sir Richard Steele's
song in the *Conscious Lovers*, about 1705, beginning, "If
Love's a sweet passion, why does it torment?" The present
song appeared also in Hogg (second series, pp. 37, 38), and he
thus annotates: "This song was both in Mr. Hardy's *MSS.*,
and in Mr. Stewart's, junr, of Dalguise. Without the variation
of a word, in the latter, it was said to have been written by Mr.
Gay" (p. 282).

Page 91. *On the Prince's picture*: See note on page 87.

,, 92. *Verses occasioned by the ringing of St. Peter's bells at Exeter on the
16 April 1748*: l. 1, *Murder will speak*, immortal Shakespeare
sung: Cf. *Hamlet*, act ii, sc. 2. This appeared in *Loyal Songs*
(as before, p. 71). Our *MS.* is corrected by its text in l. 2,
which reads badly "thou" for "though."

,, 93. *On the Execution in London & Lancashire 1716*: l. 2, *poor Jacks=*
obscure victims; l. 8, *Bid for their King a hundred thousand
pounds*. This amount actually was offered for "the Prince"
dead or alive—and not one in all Scotland of the very poorest
was found to "betray" him!

,, 96. *On the 29th May 1746*. The cherished "Birth-day" of the Jacobites—
as onward.

,, 97. *On the 10th June, by Mr David Morgan*. Our *MS.* supplies for
the first time the Author's name of this Song. Hogg printed
it and thus annotated: " Is one of the songs for the birth of
the Chevalier de St George, and seems to have been written
about the time that he came over and was crowned at Scoon.
It was copied from young Steuart of Dalguise's Collection."
(second Series, p. 282.) The Welsh authorship makes Hogg's
conjecture of the occasion improbable. The Tune is "The
King shall enjoy his own again." (Hogg, first Series, p. 1.)
Morgan is unknown to me.

,, 98. *Ode on the Victory at Gladsmuir, Septr.* 1745. This "Ode" was
printed, and copies of it (furtively) distributed, soon after the
battle it commemorates, which was fought on 21st September,
1745, and which apart from its momentary gleam of success, is
for ever associated with the death of the good Colonel Gardiner,
as told by Dr. Doddridge imperishably. It was not reprinted
in any of the earlier editions of its author's Poems — William
Hamilton of Bangour — but was, in the *Edinburgh Magazine
and Review* and in the *Scots Magazine* of 1773 — the latter in-
forming us that it had been set to music by Macgibban, cele-

brated in his day. Hogg included it in his second series (pp· 118-20). Our text seems superior to any other; but these variations may be noted : p. 98, st. 1, l. 6, "its"; p. 99, st. 2, l. 4, "In silent joy and"; l. 6, "thus to cark the"; st. 3, l. 5, "creeps"; st. 4, l. 6, "Once more I wield"; p. 100, st. 1, l. 1, "Early I"; l. 3, "I fill'd his mind with love of truth"; st. 2, l. 4, "Of generous deeds and honest toil"; st, 3, l. 6, "His single valour to an host of foes"; st. 4, l. 2, "quick-darted"; l. 5, "caught"; st. 5, l. 5, "a"; p. 101, last st., l. 1, "So shall fierce wars and tumults"; l. 2, "the"; ll. 5–6,

> "So shall these happy realms for euer proue
> The sweets of union, liberty and loue."

Hogg published this (second series, pp. 118–120).

Page 101. *Catos Ghost.* 1715. This is one of many contemporary *hits* at Addison's tragedy of "Cato."

,, 104. *Epitaph on Queen Caroline Consort to George 2d.* See on these stinging lines by Lord Chesterfield—which Earl Stanhope long sought for in vain—our Introduction. Line 7, *Tindall*, viz : Matthew Tindal, LL.D., a once celebrated Deistical Writer, born in 1657 ; died August 16, 1733.

,, 104. *Hoadley*: viz, Benjamin Hoadly, Bishop of Winchester; born 1676; died April 17, 1761.

,, 105. *The Allusion. When Israel first,* &c. Line 10, *Bishop Burnet* : one of Hogg's most trenchant Jacobite ballads is "Bishop Burnet's Descent into Hell" (first series, pp. 72–3). I quote part of his long note on it : "It is not easy to conceive what made the Jacobite party so utterly to detest Bishop Burnet, who was always a moderate man, and advised the Stuarts to moderate measures, and never in his life took any very decided part against the adherents of the abdicated family. It appears they considered him as a time-serving hypocrite. Probably it was after the publication of his Memoirs that all these bitter *jeux-d'esprit* was vented against him ; for it was always considered by the Jacobites as an unfair representation of their party that he gave in that work." (pp. 253–4.) There follows "a humourous parody of his manner and epitaph," from "a miscellany of that age." (pp. 254–57.)

,, 105. *On the Tenth of June. O. S.* = the birth-day of the Chevalier de S' George.

,, 106. *On the Tenth of June. By Mr. David Morgan.* See note on page 98.

,, 108. *A Litany for the Year* 1750. Marvell and others effectively used the form of "Litany" for pungent satire of Charles II. This *Litany* is one of the many waifs and strays (mis)assigned to

Notes and Illustrations.

Butler in his Posthumous Works (first edition, 1715, p. 43) —
The allusion to the High Court of Justice which tried and con-

Page 109. *An Acrostick on the Right Honble James Earl of Derwentwater*:
Hogg's note on his Jacobite ballad of "Derwentwater" (2nd
Series, pp. 28-30) is as follows:—"James Radcliff, Earl of
Derwentwater, was among those who met in Northumberland,
and rose in arms for King James about the beginning of October ; having been forced to that measure by warrants being past
to apprehend him and lodge him in prison, and by officers
being in search of him, whom he narrowly escaped. He was
young, and is reported to have been a beautiful and noble look-
fate drew tears from the spectators, and was a great misfortune
to the county in which he lived. He gave bread to the mul-
titudes of people, whom he employed on his estate ;—the poor,
the widow, and the orphan, rejoiced in his bounty.' This is an
269-271).

,, 110. *Great Britain's Remembrancer.* Quite distinct from this, but perhaps not unsuggested by some floating echoes of the ballad pre-

" Come listen awhile, and I'll tickle your ears,
With a few little vict'ries, by which it appears
We have gain'd from the French in two little years.
Which no body can deny, deny, &c.

We have beat them, my boys, and I'll hold you a pound,
We shall beat them, my boys, upon sea or dry ground ;
We shall beat them as long as the world goes round.
Which no body, &c.

With Guardalupe first I embellish my strain ;
Then a cluster of forts crowd into my brain,
Crown-Point, Frontenac, Niagara, Duquesne.
Which no body, &c.

Quebec we have taken, and taken Breton ;
Though the coast was so steep, that a man might as soon,
As the Frenchmen imagin'd, have taken the moon.
Which no body, &c.

Senegal we have taken, and taken Goree,
And thither we trade for our blacks, do you see,
For who should buy slaves but they that are free.
　　　Which no body, &c.

Then at Minden, you know, we defeated our foes,
Tho' our horse stood aloof without coming to blows,
And why no body's hang'd for it, no body knows.
　　　Which no body, &c.

Boscawen at Lagos, and Hawke in the Bay,
Your vict'ries had I but room to display,
I'm sure I should not have done singing to-day,
　　　Which no body, &c.

O what is become of the fleet out of Brest,
Some are burnt, some are taken, and where are the rest?
Why some are fled east, and some are fled west.
　　　Which no body, &c.

Some ten fathom deep in the sea may be found,
And some in the river Villaine are a-ground,
Where they lie very safe, but not very sound.
　　　Which no body, &c.

Let France then all title to glory resign,
For these years shall unmatch'd in our histories shine,
The renown'd *Fifty-eight*, and the great *Fifty-nine*.
　　　Which no body can deny, deny, &c.

This is transcribed from a copy printed at Whitehaven, and
dated 1771, which passed under the eyes of George Alexander
Stevens. It was, no doubt, a reprint from a London slip-song.
For the famous tune, "Which no body can deny" (an adaptation of the Elizabethan "Green-sleeves"), so much used in the
ballads against "The Rump," see Chappell's *Popular Music
of the Olden Time*, p. 233.

Page 118.　*On the Battle at Preston Pans.* Besides our text there is a second
copy, shorter and somewhat inaccurate, but supplying one or
two corrections, *e.g.*, p. 118, l. 4, "And" for "She." In l.
11, it reads "lifts his spightfull Dart"—and so here and there
verbal changes not calling for specific record.

Page 126.　l. 15, *Tabid*=wasting.

,,　129.　l. 3, *dechaise*=over-turn?

"　130.　*Declaration*, &c. See our Introduction.

,,　140.　*The Archbishop of York.*. This was Dr. Thomas Herring, who
was Archbishop from April, 1743, to October, 1747, when he
was translated to Canterbury.

　　　　　　　　　　　　　　　　　　　　A. B. G.

Printed by Charles Simms & Co., Manchester.

www.ingramcontent.com/pod-product-compliance
Lightning Source LLC
Chambersburg PA
CBHW030111030726

47498CB00007B/2338